Meet Me Under The Honeysuckle

Syren Nightshade

Disclaimers

This story is a work of fiction. Names, characters, places, and incidents are the product of the author's imagination and/or are used fictitiously. Any resemblance to actual events, locales, or persons, living or dead, is completely coincidental.

Copyright © 2022 by Syren Nightshade

The reproduction, scanning, uploading, printing, and distribution of this story without the author's permission is a theft of the author's intellectual property.

Second Edition, 2024

Cover photo by Galina Afanaseva

Content Warnings

- Adoption
- Misogyny
- Gaslighting and Controlling Behaviour

1

These were perhaps the best cookies that Agnete had ever made.

The texture was immaculate. The herbs and coarsely-ground sugar sprinkled on top was picturesque. And the taste was scientifically, mathematically, alchemically flawless. The uniformly-shaped treats would pair perfectly with her latest- and to date, favourite- blend of tea. Another recipe recently perfected.

Her triumph left her exceptionally proud and undeniably sad.

It wasn't that she didn't have anyone to share the products of her culinary prowess with. She hosted people in her home very regularly. During the busiest seasons- Beltane, mainly, and Yuletide- she would host upwards of two dozen people a week. But she never offered them food. Not out of spite, of course. If she were a more reasonable person, she might be excited at the opportunity to have a perfect batch of cookies all to herself. No, this was a matter of ethics: It was bad luck to deny a witch's hospitality.

Of all the superstitions about witches, Agnete thought that this one was among the silliest. And for her, at least, the most frustrating. It meant that, while she *could* offer her clients food and drink, they wouldn't feel comfortable saying no. They were perfectly capable of doing so- she wasn't going to hex them for turning down a light snack. But there was no telling *them* that. Beliefs about witches ran deep in this village, no matter how silly those beliefs were. And no one wants to offer refreshments to their guests if they know that their guests are going to feel coerced into taking it. So she never offered.

She got to know the names of just about everyone in the village, despite living a good distance outside of it. This was partly out of necessity, and partly another side effect of superstition: Allegedly, it was bad luck to have a witch living on the North side of your home. And the South. And depending on who you asked, potentially the West, as well. The East seemed to be rather the safest side for a magically-inclined neighbour, but it was regrettably difficult to live on the East side of someone's home without also occupying the North, South, or West side of someone else's.

At least the woods were peaceful. She was able to grow and forage for all of the ingredients she needed, and it was remarkably quiet. She had a vegetable garden and an herb garden, both of which gave her abundant harvest seasons. The animals didn't bother her much, except when they smelled something delicious cooking in her hearth. Even then, they generally waited patiently if they wanted a taste. She had spent her whole life in the woods. They knew her. They didn't fear her like they feared the other villagers. Which naturally reinforced another superstition: that witches can speak to animals and make them do their bidding.

Agnete *wished* she could speak to animals. Then at least she could have some conversation that didn't revolve around how to use a charm or a salve or a bag of herbs.

She didn't particularly enjoy being feared. For much of her life, she didn't understand it. She had always thought of herself as a warm, soft person. But this was what you had to expect, practising witchcraft in such a remote place. Before she was a witch, she was a witch's daughter. She had endured the village's suspicion her entire life. By the time her mother died, and she took up her title, she already understood that no matter how desperately she was needed, she would never be entirely trusted.

So she learned to adopt a businesslike tone with them. She learned early on that being warm and friendly made no difference- it just made them regard her with even more suspicion. At least this way, she could appear knowledgeable and competent. They only had one witch- they deserved to feel confident in her abilities. Even if she didn't always feel confident in herself.

A knock *thumped* at the door just as she was putting the cookies into a jar. She briskly crossed in front of the hearth and grabbed her shawl from the wall. She wasn't cold- it was pleasantly toasty in the small cottage. But she always wore the fringed, hand-stitched thing draped over her arms when she met with the villagers. It set her apart as a witch. It helped her get into character. Truth be told, it was more of a costume piece than anything.

When she opened the door, she had to conceal her surprise. She'd never properly spoken to the young woman before... But she recognized her. It was hard not to.

Lucia bowed her head, hiding her delicate features in a small curtsy. "Crona," she said softly, "I humbly beg aid of your wisdom."

Her voice was high and sweet, and her address perfectly polite. The standard greeting, executed with grace. Her visitor raised her face, looking at Agnete with big, expectant eyes.

Goddess, she is *beautiful.*

Lucia was universally considered to be the most beautiful woman in the village. It was easy to see why.

Just looking at here there on the doorstep was enough to start a fluttering in Agnete's stomach.

Agnete nodded solemnly and stepped aside. "Come in." Lucia wouldn't have been able to enter, otherwise. *It's bad luck to enter a witch's home uninvited.* Agnete thought this was another exceptionally silly rule. It was remarkably rude to enter *anyone's* home uninvited.

Lucia cast a modest look behind her before stepping inside, blue cloak trailing a scattering of dried, orange leaves with it over the threshold.

If rumour was to be believed, Lucia wasn't just the most beautiful woman in the village... she was practically their pride and joy. A *golden child.* Kind, gentle, pure of heart, beloved by all who meet her, et cetera, et cetera, ad nauseam.

Lucia undid the clasp of her cloak, catching Agnete's gaze with a demure, courteous smile. She folded the cloak over her arm, leaves clinging to the edge of the fabric and crinkling against her skirt. "Oh," she gasped quietly, seeing the leaves she'd tracked inside. "I'm terribly sorry."

"It's alright, I'll just sweep them out later." Agnete smiled. "Can I take your cloak?" *Damn it- I never ask that question. What's wrong with me?* Nobody trusted Agnete with their cloaks. Or scarves. Or hats. But they couldn't say no to her... *the 'hospitality' thing again.*

Lucia inclined her head again. "That would be lovely, thank you."

Not that she has a choice, now that I've asked, Agnete thought, accepting the garment. She cursed herself for her slip-up and gestured to a pair of chairs near the hearth. She tried to regain a businesslike tone. "You're welcome to sit, if you'd like."

5

"I would, thank you." Lucia perched herself into the seat. As Agnete turned to drape the cloak over a nearby hook tree, she heard Lucia say, "You have a lovely home... It must be peaceful, living so far into the forest. The walk here was beautiful. But... perhaps a little long. Could I trouble you for a cup of tea?"

Agnete almost tripped over her own feet. *She... asked me for tea.*

Nobody asked her for tea.

Never mind that the request was masterfully made, opened with both a compliment and an invitation to talk about herself. *She* asked me *for tea.*

She struggled to contain the wave of excitement that washed over her. "Of course." She had never had the chance to share her creations with anyone. Not since her mother, anyways.

It didn't take long to brew the pot of tea- her latest blend- and pour it into a pair of handleless cups. Neither of them spoke. It felt awkward, but Agnete decided that she would take silence over letting her excitement get the better of her. She glanced at the jar of freshly-baked cookies. *Should I risk it?*

It was far too tempting. Zeal overcame her reservations, and she arranged a half-dozen cookies onto a saucer.

She brought the offerings to Lucia, placing them on a small table between them.

"Thank you," Lucia said. She reached for the cup, but retracted her fingers as soon as she touched it, the whisper of a wince causing her lip to twitch.

"Sorry... It's still hot."

"Of course."

Agnete opened her mouth to ask if she'd like a sleeve for her cup... then cleared her throat, catching herself. *'Hospitality'. Right.* She shifted back into her chair- she was usually more collected than this. *"Golden girl" indeed... Even her presence is disarming.* "How can I aid you?"

Lucia shifted in the chair. She crossed her legs. The doe-eyed expression that she had been wearing since she arrived fell away from her face like a shroud. When she spoke, she did so with a jarringly direct tone. "I need a sleeping potion. A powerful one. And a lot of it."

Agnete blinked. *What... is happening?* It was though she was suddenly talking to a completely different person. "May I... ask what this potion is for?"

"Sleeping," she answered, deadpan.

"Yes, of course... But..."

"It's for my husband."

Agnete could feel herself paling. *Oh, dear.* She hadn't even realized that Lucia had been married. "...Have you been married to your husband for very long?"

"No."

...Oh dear. "...There is certainly something," she answered carefully, "that would fit your needs... for *sleeping*, that is-" she prayed it was sleeping- "But I would recommend something more... mild, to start with."

" *'Mild'?* "

"If something mild doesn't work, then perhaps we could gradually-"

"I need something strong. The strongest you can possibly give me."

She was determined. Agnete tried to hide the way her fingers started searching for something to fidget with. It always made her endlessly uncomfortable when she had to tell people that she wouldn't be an accessory to murder. "You know, a remedy of that strength... It would be enough to cause death, given the wrong dose-"

"I know."

"Then-"

"I'm not trying to kill my husband, if that's what you're asking."

It unequivocally *was* what Agnete was asking. *But she didn't have to be so blunt about it.* "Then... If I may ask-"

"You can give it to me in regular, small doses, if you like," she cut her off. "If it would put your mind at rest."

Considering how easy it would be for you to stockpile it... No. It would not. But she was staring so unflinchingly at Agnete that it made her want to squirm in her seat. "Very well..." *It's a start.* "The matter of price, however..."

"I'm not expecting it to be cheap."

It wouldn't be. A concoction that powerful would require herbs that were very scarce in the area, and- as an added measure of safety- would need to be treated in a very specific way before being dried, to reduce their potency. It would still be lethal in a big enough dose, but Agnete certainly wasn't going to give her the full potency if she could help it. *She won't know any different.*

"It won't be," Agnete confirmed. "Not only are the materials scarce, but they will require much time and effort to process. Additionally, I wouldn't *just* be providing you with a sleeping aid... I would be providing you with the means to end someone's life, should you choose to." She tried to sound as foreboding as she could. "That *alone* is worth more than mere coins."

"I'll pay you whatever you want."

Agnete took a breath. *Okay. Here it comes.*

Part of her hoped that hearing the cost of what she was asking for would make her change her mind. Part of her wondered if she was even *ready* to ask this of Lucia... of *anyone*. It would be the first time she'd ever asked it. Her mother had told her that it was good to wait until you were ready, but to get the first time out of the way early. Most people said *no* to an exchange like this... which, quite frankly, was fair. But balance was the law of nature, and the law of witchcraft.

"There is only one way to pay for the power of death... and that is with the promise of life."

"Very well."

Agnete straightened in her chair and met Lucia's eyes. *This is it... the big moment.*

I wish you could see it, Mom.

"In exchange for this remedy," Agnete said, "you will give me your firstborn child."

"Done."

Agnete blinked. The speed and certainty with which she answered was... *alarming.*

There must be a reason. It was a common occurrence for people to try and trick witches into accepting a payment that they had no intention of making.

She swallowed. "You... I trust you are *able* to bear children, to the best of your knowledge?"

"To the best of my knowledge, yes."

"And... you do *intend* on having children, in the future?"

"Yes, I presume that I will."

Well, now... this is a riddle. "You have not already *had* a child?"

"No."

"And you are not currently with child?" *It would make sense for her to make the deal, if she had accidentally conceived a child she wasn't ready for.*

"I am not."

"It is *very* bad luck to lie to a witch."

"I'm sure it is."

Agnete inhaled sharply and leaned back into her chair, at a loss for words. "...Well."

Lucia reached for her cup again, only to find it still too hot. She grimaced, looking annoyed at the heat on her fingers. Agnete got up and retrieved a knitted sleeve for the cup, if only to take the edge off of her nervous energy.

"None of your cups have handles?" Lucia asked as she slipped the handmade sleeve over the cup.

"No. I like them better this way. You get to wrap your hands around it. It's cozy."

"Burning your fingers is *cozy.*"

"Well... you get used to it."

Lucia made a skeptical noise as Agnete sat back down. "Thank you," she said, picking up the cup and bringing it to her lips. She paused as the tea hit her tongue. Agnete waited for a comment... but she wordlessly replaced the cup on the table. "Actually-"

Agnete perked up. *This is it,* she thought. *This is where she reconsiders.* She knew her assent was given too quickly.

"What if I have twins?"

Agnete raised an eyebrow. "It would be your *first* born... Whichever twin was born first."

"And if the child is unsatisfactory to you in some way?"

"They're a child, how can they be 'unsatisfactory'?"

"I don't know what you want the child for."

"To *raise*, what else would I want them for?"

"Their personality or abilities might not suit your aims."

"I have no aims."

"Then why do you want the child?" Lucia abruptly shook her head and waved her hand. "Never mind. It's none of my business." Agnete bristled. *'None of your business'?* "What if the child is stillborn? Or dies in the cradle?"

Agnete tried very hard to maintain her composure in the face of Lucia's rapid-fire questions. "If their death is your doing... then I *will* come for you. And you *will* pay." It was a threat that fell readily from her tongue. "But if their death is accidental, or out of your control..." she shrugged. "That's unfortunate for me."

"Do I have to give them to you right away?"

"Not necessarily. It's up to my discretion."

"And if you're unable to hold up your end of the arrangement?"

Agnete hesitated. She hadn't expected this question. She didn't even think she'd heard anyone ask her *mother* this question. Lucia was staring at her, waiting for an answer. Her fingers found the edge of her shawl as she tried to suppress a nervous titter. "...I could give you *my* firstborn?"

Lucia's brow furrowed. "Why the hell would I want your firstborn?"

She stuttered. "It... It was a joke. Um." *Mother did not prepare me for this.*

"I mean, if you aren't able to provide the sleeping aid for the agreed upon length of time... Or if you aren't able to provide the agreed upon *amount*..."

Well, you'll still have to pay for what you did *receive.* "You will owe me a favour instead of your firstborn. Anything I ask. No matter how big or how small. You *must* grant it to me." If all else failed, she could use that favour to keep her from killing her husband. If not... favours were always handy.

"So, to be clear," Lucia said, taking another sip of her tea, "I'll receive an effective amount of this... *potion?*"

"Herbs."

"-*Herbs*. Over an ongoing period of time, on a... *twice weekly?*"

"Weekly."

"-*Weekly* basis. If you're unable to provide, then I'll owe you a single favour for what you *have* given me. One that I can't say no to. Otherwise, I will give you my firstborn child in exchange for the agreed upon amount of herbs."

Agnete gulped. "Yes-"

"Done."

She blinked. "...O...Okay."

"I'm sure you need time to prepare," Lucia said over the rim of her cup. "When can I expect my first batch?"

Agnete knew where to find some of the herbs, which would give her a good head start on the foraging end of things... But she did need time to treat and dry them. If she got started tonight... "A week?"

"A week, then."

"Shall I deliver them to you?"

Lucia shook her head. "No. I'll come here." She downed the rest of her tea and rose from her seat. Agnete followed her lead, glancing down at the plate of cookies.

"...Would you like a cookie?" She felt silly asking. But seeing them untouched made her a little sad.

"No, thank you. Every time I go to the baker, they inundate me with extra sweets that I never ask for. Between that and all of the sweets gifted to me by neighbours who want to get into my good graces, I get sick of sugar rather quickly." Agnete tried to hide her disappointment. *At least she's not afraid to say no... That's more than I can say for everyone else.* "That tea was delicious, though."

Agnete's heart started pitter-pattering in her chest. "Oh?"

"It was, actually... *very* delicious." She heard the honey start to return to Lucia's voice. "The herbs are important, but I may need to get some of that tea from you, as well!"

"I might have to charge you extra," Agnete joked as Lucia re-fastened her cloak over her shoulders.

"How about my second-born?" Lucia asked lightly.

Agnete looked at her, feeling the colour rise to her cheeks. Lucia returned the look, her sweet smile never leaving her face.

I can't tell if she's joking or not.

She turned to leave, gasping suddenly as she opened the door. "Oh!" she said. "If anyone asks about our arrangement... or if anyone says *anything*... you tell them *nothing.*"

She walked out the door, leaving Agnete to deal with a quickly-growing wave of anxiety.

Goddess, please... don't let this woman be a murderer.

2

"You know, I didn't actually get your name last time we met."

It was true. She hadn't asked Agnete for her name.

Lucia had just walked through her door for the second time, dropping her façade just as quickly as she had the first. Agnete had the herbs tucked into a small drawstring bag, ready to go.

"It's Agnete." *At least she asked.* Most of the villagers didn't bother to. If they had to address her, they just used *Crona.*

"*Agnete,*" Lucia repeated. "Like *Agnete Bloodmoon?*"

Agnete Bloodmoon, Witch of the mist; Met a great wolf and gave him her kiss... She was, unfortunately, familiar with the rhyme. Village children had used it to taunt her, when she was small. The story told of a witch who came across a wolf trapped in the forest. After she freed him from the trap, she kissed him, magically transforming him into a man. It's said that he became her protector- and, depending on who you asked, her lover. There were countless ways to interpret the piece of folklore. Agnete rarely ever heard the kinder ones. "No," she answered. "It was my Mother's Mother's name."

"The one who birthed you, or the one who raised you?" Lucia stepped over to a small table, examining a small vase in front of the window with curiosity. The vase held a lanky plant cutting, propagating in the sun. The small, pink-purple flowers trembled as Lucia slipped her fingers under a leaf.

Agnete cringed at the question. It wasn't impolite, exactly. Just... direct. "Both. I'm actually her natural daughter."

Lucia turned her attention towards Agnete and frowned. "I thought witches *took* children?"

"*Adopt them,* yes... But not all of us. And not all of the people who need our services are able to bear children. And we can't very well *force their partners* to bear children. So sometimes, in lieu of their firstborn, a client may pay with their..." She coughed uncomfortably.

"Their seed," Lucia said flatly.

"Yes... And, well..." Agnete shrugged.

Lucia appeared to consider this. "...I see. And this is how you were born."

"Yes."

"Do you ever wonder who your father was?"

The corner of Agnete's mouth twitched as she considered the question. "Occasionally? But not really," she answered. "Mostly just idle curiosity."

"That would drive me *mad.*"

Her brow furrowed. "Why?"

"I'd just hate not knowing," Lucia said simply.

"And yet you're willing to do the same thing to your firstborn child?"

The words were out of her mouth before she could think to stop them. The icy look on Lucia's face made Agnete pale. Her mouth suddenly felt very dry. *Oh, dear... That was a mistake. That was a horrifically rude mistake.* It hadn't been intended as a judgment... But that wasn't going to help her, now.

Agnete opened her mouth to apologize, but Lucia grabbed the small bag of herbs from her hands and made for the door. "I'll be back next week," she said, sharp enough to make Agnete wince.

The door slammed shut behind her. The kettle started to boil behind her.

At least I put the dosage instructions in the bag.

3

When Lucia stepped into her home again, she stopped and stood stiffly at the door.

Agnete didn't blame her.

"...I'm... Sorry about last week," she told Lucia. "Living alone in the woods doesn't give me many chances to practice my social skills. I shouldn't have asked you that. About your child."

Lucia's shoulders relaxed. "...It's fine," she said after a long pause. "It was a valid question." Stepping away from the door and surrendering herself into a chair on the porch, she added, "I'm not just a horrible person, you know. I'm not just giving away a child for no reason."

"I never said-"

"I know. But..." Her breath comes out in a frustrated *huff*. "The sleeping herbs are for my husband. For *actual* sleeping. He's an insomniac."

"...You must really love him," she replied carefully.

Lucia surprised her by actually snorting. "*No*. He seems very taken with *me,* though."

Sympathy crept readily into Agnete's chest. She stepped over the threshold and leaned against the wall. "I'm sorry. Were you forced into the marriage?" She couldn't imagine why else Lucia would have married a man she didn't love. *She could have her pick of anyone in the village.*

"No," she answered shortly. "Growing up, my parents wouldn't let me do anything. Learn valuable skills, study, travel anywhere... I was too beautiful and graceful a girl to ruin with labour or complicated ideas. I was stuck learning the *'feminine'* arts. Sewing, embroidery, baking, singing... Skills that were meant for others to enjoy. To serve my future husband, my children, the guests I would host at pretty little parties at my pretty little home. Useless skills, meant to serve everyone but myself."

Agnete blushed. *I love doing all of those things. I don't think they're useless at all.* Still, she tried to see it from Lucia's perspective. *It wasn't what she wanted. None of it was. She probably wanted to feel clever and capable, and all she got was feeling delicate and useless.*

"The 'chaste' part was easy for me to play," Lucia continued, situating herself into the chair she occupied during her first visit. "Not because I never desired anyone. But because I knew lovers were distractions. So I remained unattached for as long as I could. Eventually, though, my family became anxious to see me settle down." Her voice took on a bitter edge. "What use is a beautiful daughter if she can't be a wife and a mother, right?"

"So you married to appease them?"

"Well... yes. And no." Agnete darted smoothly into the house as Lucia spoke, listening as she took the teapot and pair of mugs from the mantle. "I'm not blind. I know what I look like. I know I can have almost any man I want. And when Bartrand made his interest clear-" her back sank into the cushioned chair- "It was a perfect opportunity."

Bartrand... I've heard that name before... Who is that? As she put the tea on the small table between them and poured into the sleeved cup, it hit her. *Goddess... She's married the mayor. The single most powerful man in the entire village.* She suddenly felt a strange sort of self-consciousness. "There wasn't anyone else you felt more affection for?" Agnete asked, ducking back inside.

"There was... there had been. But I had to be realistic. I have goals. And Bartrand was by far the best prospect. He has status, which gives me some social authority. He has money. He's older than me. Old enough to value companionship over lust, and old enough to die well before I do- barring any ill fortune befalling me, of course. But he's not so old that he's likely to die before I'm prepared to be widowed. And most importantly, he has an extensive private library."

The savoury vegetable, herb, & cheese tarts had joined the tea on the table before Lucia had even finished talking. They had only emerged from the oven two hours ago. "What do you like to read?"

"Anything. Everything." Her eyes seem to cloud over, just a little. "This village is a terrible little place. Books are a refuge. They're an escape. I often feel like losing myself in a story is the only thing that keeps me sane. Every other minute of the day, when I'm not reading something, I feel trapped here."

Agnete wondered a lot of things as she finally gave herself permission to sit next to Lucia. Primarily, *If you want to leave so badly, why not just leave?* What she asked instead was, "Why do you need the sleeping herbs?"

"As I said," Lucia replied, wrapping her fingers over the sleeved cup, "My husband is an insomniac. Sleep does not come easily to him. Sometimes, it doesn't come at all. And while he's at home in the evenings, he is either in his library, or with me. But never both at the same time. He will not allow *me* into his library."

"He doesn't permit you to read?"

"That either, no. If I want to read, I need to do it while he's out of the house, or asleep. And since he leaves all of the cooking, *and* the cleaning, *and* the housework to me," she sneers, "I have no time during the day. So I only have one option."

"The herbs?"

Lucia nods. "As far as he's concerned, every night we have a ritual, just the two of us: I brew him his nightly tea- the same he's had every night since he was a child, just like his mother used to make. As far as *he* knows, at least. And after I bring him his tea, sweetened with milk, just the way he likes it, I take his head on my lap, and he tells me of his many, trivial little troubles. And I pet his head, just like an old dog- and he *is* like a dog, for the drool he occasionally leaves on my dress- and I *'sing him to sleep'* with a few pithy little lullabies." She takes a sip of her tea. "And so he is endeared to me... the only woman in the whole *world* who can put his head and his heart to rest." Agnete suppressed a small grimace. *It sounds like you're just taking credit for* my *work,* she thought, *but very well.* "I go into his big, beautiful library and read whatever I wish to while he sleeps, and he remains wrapped around my dainty little finger."

"I... *see.*" *When does* she *sleep?*

Lucia paused. "...You don't approve." It sounded more like a statement than a question.

Agnete shook her head. "It's not that." Truthfully, she didn't fully know what 'it' was.

It's just that I'm unnerved by your blunt cunning. And that I still admire your honesty with me, anyways. And that I'm wondering if I should feel sympathy for your husband. But I already feel so much sympathy for you, *so plainly resentful of the cage you've been put in. And instead of escaping it, you've locked yourself inside.*

A wayward breeze blew floral debris over their feet. Fallen leaves tumbled leisurely across the porch while deep magenta petals made a lovely, haphazard mess around their shoes. Lucia glanced to her left, towards the bush from whence they came.

"...Dahlias?" she asked.

"Close," Agnete replied. "Most people know them as nightblush. They don't grow very close to the village, anymore... too many people. I think they've all been dug up or overpicked. But there are still some bushes out here. It's actually what you were looking at yesterday." When Lucia furrowed her brows, Agnete added, "The cutting in the vase?"

"Oh. *Oh!* Yes, I remember."

"They're very pretty. I can give you one, if you'd like?" The very one she was looking at the previous week, specifically.

A small smile escaped Lucia. "I would like that." She cast another glance outwards, across the garden and into the trees. A pair of squirrels chased each other up a nearby trunk, gradually becoming a playful, twisting mass of fluff in the branches. Birds spoke to one another in the distance, chirps filling the space between the rustling leaves.

Lucia swallowed. "When you asked me for my firstborn..." she sighed and looked down into her lap. "You... seem like you'd give a child a good home. Like you'd make a good mother. Not like me. So if giving my child a happy home is the price I pay for keeping my sanity until I'm able to leave this place... So be it."

Agnete's throat hitched a little. *A good mother.* She hazarded a glance at Lucia- her eyes were still downcast.

Lucia peered into the mug held on her lap. She hesitated. "You know... It's nice not having to wear a mask with someone."

The words settled on Agnete like a heavy blanket. People she barely knew would dump all of their repressed feelings and secret desires at her feet, sometimes, when they came to her asking for help. And she didn't mind... truly. But no one had ever faced her with such unadorned honesty before. Honesty devoid of desperation, shame, or hyperbole. No one had ever really *talked* to her.

The fireplace crackled quietly beside them, sending tiny cinders into the air. Her fingertips ran over the ridges of her cup. She looked back at Lucia. "It's nice just having somebody talk to me."

4

"-Which reminds me," Lucia said between bites of tea sandwich, "I can't come here, anymore."

Something in Agnete sank a little bit. "Oh." After the terseness of Lucia's first couple of visits had relaxed, Agnete had started looking forward to spending time together. She had quickly forgotten just how blunt Lucia could be. "Did you not need the herbs, anymore?"

Lucia chortled. "Of course I still need them- I haven't found a way out of this village, yet. *Regrettably.* No, I just can't come out here to retrieve them, anymore. My husband is..." she made a sound somewhere between a groan and a sigh. "He's... a very *insecure* man. He knows I'm slipping off into the woods every week and doesn't know why. He won't accuse me of seeing another man outright... But I can tell that the seed is planted. Or, more aptly, the seed is being *watered.*"

Agnete made a face. "So he's possessive."

"Yes and no. His actions aren't driven by wanting to *possess me,* per se. They're more driven by him projecting his own insecurities onto everyone around him. But that hardly matters- the consequences to me are the same."

"So... he feels inferior?"

"Ultimately, yes. He fears that he isn't good enough, or smart enough, or desirable enough. He hides it well, I'll give him that. But he's constantly afraid of losing what he has- I think- to someone who *'deserves it more'.* And because- whether he admits it or not- he believes himself unworthy, he's afraid of everyone else discovering just how unworthy he is. Which is supposed to be his little secret. So any potential threat- *the threat of being found out as unworthy,* that is- is met with hostility." She takes another big sip of tea. "That usually means keeping me uncomfortably close, where I can give him plenty of reassurance. Naturally, he gets rather antsy when I seem too friendly with other men."

"Lucia..." Agnete put her cup on the table and leaned forward. "That's... not okay."

Lucia met her gaze unflinchingly. The spritely flames from the hearth reflected in the corners of her eyes. Agnete waited, searched for some small crack behind them.

Lucia's fingers suddenly jumped gracefully to her lips. She giggled.

"You are...*sweet*," she said, stifling her laugh. Agnete blushed. "You forget that I'm the one using *him*. I discerned all of this before I decided to marry him. But," she added soberly, "Your heart is in the right place... If it were somebody else..." she shook her head. "Better me than another girl."

Agnete picked up her cup again and hid behind the rim as she took a sip. *I still don't like the idea of you living like that,* she thought.

Lucia must have seen her face, for she said, "It's alright, sweetling. I'm more than capable of handling him."

Something in Agnete's stomach fluttered. "If there's one thing you are," she said, "It's capable. I mean- I *imagine*. I guess I wouldn't really know... But you seem capable. Especially if you could figure all of that out about Bartrand before you married him. Not that it automatically means you're able to handle him- theory and practice are two different beasts- but I'm sure you can do that, too-" she struggled to stop her rambling as a small smile played on Lucia's face.

"Either way," Lucia said, mercifully interrupting her, "If I keep coming out here, he'll only grow more suspicious. And I can't afford that. So you'll have to come to me."

"...Oh."

"It's fine," she replied with a dismissive wave of her hand. "I've thought this through. You making regular house calls to me would look strange... I'm not discernibly sick. People would talk." She leaned back into her chair. "I have a plan. All you need to do is follow my lead."

Agnete eyed the bundles of herbs drying high around the hearth; each one was tied with twine and dangling from a small hook in a low beam. If she concentrated, she could find their scents hiding between layers of hearthsmoke and the morning's baking. She was tempted to ask what this *'plan'* was. And why it was even necessary.

This doesn't have to be so complicated.

"Alright."

Lucia took a sip of her tea. As she dropped the cup back onto the table, she opened her mouth to speak, only to stop short of the first word. She stared past Agnete. "You seem to have another guest."

Agnete turned to look over her shoulder. A chipmunk was wandering across the kitchen table, sniffing at forgotten crumbs. Agnete smiled at them. "It's alright. They're friendly."

Lucia made a face. "You just let them into the house?"

"Of course I do, don't be silly."

"*'Don't be silly'*? There is a wild animal *in your house.*"

"It's just a chipmunk. It's not a bear."

"It's *in your house.*"

The corner of Agnete's lip pinched. "Is that strange?"

"Yes...?"

She had never thought to question it. Her mother had always let the odd chipmunk, squirrel, or bird wander their home.

As the rodent climbed down the leg of the table and wandered over, Agnete tore a small piece of bread off of her sandwich. She bent in her seat, extending the morsel towards the chipmunk. The chipmunk approached and took the offering, tiny paws tickling the tips of Agnete's fingers. As they stuffed the bread in their mouth, Agnete caught Lucia staring, perplexed.

"You can feed them, if you want," she told her.

"...Is that sanitary?"

Agnete shrugged. "I've been doing it my entire life, and it's never made me sick." When she saw Lucia hesitating, Agnete tore another piece off of her sandwich and offered it to her. "Try it."

Lucia regarded it with restrained curiosity. Setting her jaw, she took the food and immediately leaned down to offer it to the chipmunk.

"Careful, don't move too quickly," Agnete told her.

The chipmunk sniffed the air before haltingly making their way towards Lucia's hand. Lucia didn't flinch as they leaned across her open palm to reach for the food. They lingered at the very tips of her fingers as they ate, and Lucia's attempt to suppress the smile hiding behind her lips relented.

Agnete brought her empty cup to her own lips and pretended to drink. She wasn't as skilled at hiding her smiles as Lucia.

5

Agnete adjusted her shawl about her shoulders. There was a slight chill in the air, and the mist that hung between the spindly trees seemed to cling to her just as much as it did the leaves. She hitched up her skirt to avoid trailing it through the mud as she walked.

She didn't make the trip into the village often. It was a long walk, and the way people looked at her made her feel uneasy. *Unwelcome.* She preferred it when they didn't bother looking at her at all. Every time her feet passed from the dirt path of the woods to the cobbled streets, she longed for the blissful ignorance she had as a child. She didn't notice how people looked at her and her mother, then. She hadn't noticed the other parents keeping their children close as she traipsed through puddles, strained her neck marvelling up at the village's tall clock tower, and shouted & whistled into wells, just to hear how her voice echoed against the stone.

Now, she kept her eyes on the damp stone street beneath her as she took measured steps between narrow, two-storey homes and through the village square. If she counted her steps, she could almost forget the feeling of eyes on her as she walked. She caught a whiff of something spiced as she passed one of the stalls in the square- she tried to stop herself from salivating. There always seemed to be an undercurrent of smoke in the air, here; she found it comforting despite her unease.

She found Lucia's home- or rather, her husband's home- easily enough. She didn't live within its bounds, but the streets and corners of the village were still familiar to Agnete. The Mayor's house was difficult to miss. Though not a sprawling estate by any stretch, it was, as Lucia had so succinctly put it, *"the big one"*.

She used the knocker- polished brass- and waited. Lucia swung open the door, a beam of something bright in defiance of the dreary day. "Oh good, you're here!"

Agnete was pulled inside before she could say so much as a quick hello. The brightly-lit, dark-wooded hallway was all she had the chance to see before she was drawn into the parlour and in front of a nervous man she didn't immediately recognize.

"Agnete, you know Yannis?"

The whirlwind abduction into the house had unhinged her composure. "The name sounds familiar-?" she offered.

The man rose hastily. "You aided my mother a few years ago, Crona, with a stomach ailment she was suffering from."

The name was coming back to her, now. *Yannis*- "Helen's son, yes, of course. I do remember. How is she?" *That is what one asks, isn't it? 'How is your mother?'*

"Dead," Yannis replied, then added, stuttering, "But not from your remedy, of course, Crona! Or the illness. You helped her tremendously! No, she... passed of something else. Not the stomach illness. Or by your hand, of course!"

Agnete stood stiff in awkward hesitation. "...*Good,*" she managed to say after a long pause.

Despite Lucia standing right next to her, the situation suddenly felt wildly out of her control. She was too paralyzed to clarify that she wasn't, in fact, *glad* to hear of Yannis's mother's passing.

Lucia's pleasant smile, predictably, never left her face. "Why don't you two get acquainted while I fetch the refreshments?"

Agnete fought to keep herself from physically grabbing onto her hostess like a life raft. She couldn't bear the thought of a minute alone with this poor, uneasy man who she all but congratulated on his loss. "Why don't I come help you?" she asked her.

"That won't be-"

"Please, I insist," Agnete said as she nearly pushed Lucia out of the room.

In the kitchen, Agnete tried to restrain herself to a whisper. *"What is going on?!"*

Lucia's mask dropped as quickly as it always did. "I'm setting you up," she replied, as though it were obvious. "At least, as far as the rest of the village is concerned. Or not. It could be real, if you're interested-"

"This was your plan? To play matchmaker?"

"I mean..." Lucia picked up a plate of sweets and gestured with it. "What's wrong with Yannis? He's kind enough. He shares a certain... *gentleness,* with you. He's honest."

Agnete exercised her *'gentleness'* in removing the plate from Lucia's hand and planting it firmly on the butcher's block between them. She stared at her, trying and failing to will the colour from her cheeks.

"...Maybe he wouldn't be my *first* choice, for the adoptive father of my future child," Lucia eventually relented, "But considering the selection of local bachelors, I suppose they could do worse-"

"I-" Agnete sighed. "I'm really not comfortable with this."

"Do you not like him?"

"As a person, he's... fine. I'm sure. I just... don't like *hims. Any hims.*"

"...*Oh,*" Lucia replied. "I see... Should I try to find a... an agreeable *her,* or-?"

Agnete fidgeted with the edge of her shawl. *"No...* no, that's... really not necessary."

An ambiguous silence passed between them. Agnete braved a glance at Lucia's face; she couldn't tell what she was thinking. After a minute, Lucia seemed to return from her thoughts.

"I'm sorry I didn't ask you first," she said.

"It's alright."

"We should bring Yannis his tea and cookies."

Agnete hummed in thoughtful agreement. "I suppose we really should... We wouldn't want to be rude," she added, cringing.

"Yes... Would you take the tea out for me? I'll bring the cookies in a moment."

Agnete put the pot, cups, and saucers on a service tray and did as she was asked.

-

It was funny, Agnete noted later, after she and Lucia had migrated back into the kitchen. *It was funny how Lucia took her tea.*

When they were in Agnete's cottage, she drank it black. But sitting with guests, expertly guiding the ebbs and flows of smalltalk, she had gone so far as to take her tea with generous helpings of cream and sugar. *She plays the part down to the finest details.*

After a lengthy digression between her and Lucia, Yannis had dozed off in his chair. Agnete couldn't blame him- not after her own misstep earlier. And not when the room was so comfortably and attentively kept, the soft, dependable *tick, tick, tick* of a clock on the mantle punctuating the meandering of time.

The two of them sat now in the kitchen, having left Yannis to his nap in the parlour. They sat at the butcher's block, stools pulled up right to the edge of the surface, a pair of deep blue teacups and a gradually emptying platter of cookies between them. Lucia had waved the sweets away and encouraged Agnete to enjoy as many of them as she liked. It was an offer that Agnete, with her fondness for sweets, was delighted to take advantage of. She was so used to making her own treats. Sampling those of another baker felt oddly indulgent.

"So... How did you know?" Lucia asked. Agnete gave her a quizzical look. "That you didn't like *hims*," she clarified.

Agnete swallowed the cookie she had been savouring. "Oh..."

"If it's not too personal, of course, I wouldn't want to pry."

"No, no, that's alright," she replied. She thought about how to answer. "Well... I guess I just always knew? My mother never assumed anything, so it was easy to just... be."

"That must have been nice." There was something cold hiding behind Lucia's voice. "Having a parent that never assumed."

Agnete studied her. Her shoulders seemed to sink since the last time she looked at her. She was looking through the bottom of her empty teacup, one finger threaded through the ceramic handle. *Assumptions are heavy things to bear, aren't they?*

"I'm sorry," Lucia said abruptly. "I didn't mean to turn this into another conversation about myself."

"That's fine," Agnete said. "I don't mind." *'I like hearing about you,'* she almost said. *I've spent my whole life living in the same little house in the trees. My closest friend was my own mother. I do the exact same things every day. You're far more interesting than I am.*

Lucia hesitated. "I guess... I always just assumed that everyone liked... *anyone.* There were one or two boys that I liked, growing up. And one or two girls. But I didn't realize that most people weren't like that. I didn't realize until I was... twelve, maybe? Give or take. Then I just... started questioning all of the feelings I had for other girls. Because they always felt different from the feelings I had for boys. Still romantic feelings, but... not exactly the same *kind* of romantic feelings. And I started to think that meant that they weren't really romantic, at all."

You poor thing, Agnete thought. *There's a difference between questioning what you don't yet know about yourself, and being made to question what you already know to be true.* "I'm so sorry. That must have been isolating."

Lucia nodded haltingly, raising her hand to her chin as if to hide it. "I haven't wanted many people. But those I have... I suppose it doesn't matter. I haven't wanted any of them *nearly* as much as I want to leave this place."

So why don't you? "Do you ever get lonely?"

Lucia shakes her head. "It doesn't matter. I'll have plenty of time to fall in love after I've escaped here."

Somehow, Agnete wasn't convinced. *Will that truly be enough for you?*

"Do you ever get lonely?" Lucia asked, "Living the life you do?"

Yes. Of course she did. But she didn't want to say it. Agnete's eyes darted away, and she blinked over her shoulder. "Should we check on Yannis?"

"He's still asleep."

"Are you sure? I'd hate to be rude, especially since you brought him here just to talk to me-"

"Trust me," Lucia replied bluntly, "He's asleep."

Something in her delivery didn't sit right with Agnete. Then it dawned on her. "Lucia... *you didn't.*"

"I put a pinch of the herbs in his food. After you told me you weren't interested."

Agnete sputtered. "You can't just *poison* people!"

"It's not *poison*, it's for sleeping. Don't be dramatic."

"It's poison in the wrong dose!"

"I didn't use the wrong dose. In fact, I used an excessively *correct* dose."

"You can't just *sedate* people! You can't just put them to sleep because you don't want to talk to them anymore!"

"You were uncomfortable. And he's tedious. I wanted to spend more time talking. Just the two of us."

Agnete continued to protest despite the little warm feeling in her chest. "Wh- he's going to remember-"

"-That we were having a comfortably dull exchange when he nodded off. It'll be fine. This way, at least, if you don't want to talk to him again, you can just pretend to be offended that he fell asleep on us."

"*This was so. Unnecessary.*"

"I just gave you a *perfect* out-"

"Of a problem that *you* created!"

Lucia looked her over, insufferably calm. She nudged the plate of cookies towards her. "...Take some cookies home with you and call it even?"

Agnete looked down at the plate. Then suspiciously up at Lucia.

"*I didn't put anything on them!*"

"I truly *cannot* believe you."

6

"I've been wondering about the child thing."

"Oh?" Agnete's teacup clinked back onto its saucer.

Her shawl lay neatly folded by the fireplace, close enough for it to be warm when she needed to venture back out into the cool afternoon. It rested on top of a book that Lucia had insisted on lending her. *'Bartrand won't even notice that it's missing,'* she had told her. *'And it's too beautiful a story not to be shared.'* On a nearby end table, squarely in front of the window, sat the nightblush cutting that Agnete had gifted to Lucia. Agnete thought it looked out of place- the only living, imperfect thing in a room full of elegant, strategically placed furniture and precisely folded textiles. *'Bartrand wanted it in the kitchen,'* Lucia had mentioned, *'in the cabinet, stuffed behind the glass. But it was wilting there, not getting enough light or air. And it gets so chilly at night, with the window not wanting to close properly. So I moved it here. He pouted about it, of course. But I bat my eyelashes a few times and he yielded.'*

Lucia's husband was out again, and she hadn't bothered to take out the cream or sugar for the tea Agnete brought over. A plate of snacks sat between them- tiny rolls of herbed bread, tomatoes, and sharp cheese, fresh from Agnete's kitchen were stacked primly next to a half-eaten pile of ginger cakes gifted to Lucia the previous day.

"The entire idea is to raise the child to be your successor, yes?" Lucia asked. "What do you do if the child isn't suited to it? Or just refuses?"

"Well, we never *force* a child to follow in our footsteps..." Agnete shifted in her seat. "In fact, we generally end up raising several children before we have one that will choose to succeed us."

"What happens to the ones who don't become witches?"

"What do you mean?"

"I mean, what happens?" Lucia's brow furrows. "Do you give them away?"

The *matter-of-fact* tone in her voice left Agnete more incredulous than the question itself did. "*Goddess, no!*" She fought to keep her hand from her chest. Her answer came out sounding more like a series of scandalized questions. "We *raise* them? Because... they're our children? And... that's what we signed up for?"

Lucia's eyes narrowed. "Like a... *regular* family?"

"Yes, of course!"

"So... for all intents and purposes... they *are* your own children?"

"Yes."

Lucia considered the idea. Agnete tried to compose herself as she watched her lift the cup to her lips and take a pensive sip. "If you only have one child at a time," she said slowly, "One could easily go their entire life raising potential successors, only to die without one."

"It's not uncommon for witches to have more than one child at a time. Two, three... sometimes- *but rarely-* more. They just grow up like any other siblings do."

Lucia leaned forward. "I see. Did you have any siblings?"

"No. I was an only child."

"Did you *want* siblings?"

"I suppose siblings would have been nice, but-" guilt caught Agnete's throat. *Mom gave me everything. I can't possibly ask this of her ghost.* She swallowed the rest of the words. "I suppose that would have been nice."

Lucia's head tilted faintly to one side. "You seem sad."

"I was just thinking about my mother." Agnete's finger caressed the handle of her teacup, sliding over the blue ceramic, threading itself through the hole. The glaze felt too smooth, almost slippery under her skin. She wanted traction- something to ground her. "I miss her."

"I'm sorry. I heard of it, when she passed away. How long ago was that...?" she asked herself.

"It's been a few years, now," Agnete answered. "Almost six."

"And she was your only family?"

Agnete nodded. She could feel Lucia's eyes on her. It felt as though she were looking right through her. But then, she suspected that she would have felt this way if *anyone* had got her talking about her mother.

"That sounds... lonely," Lucia replied. Agnete hadn't noticed that Lucia was leaning even further in now, almost as though she was about to get out of the chair and walk over to her. She certainly *spoke* as though they were nearer to each other than they were. "I'm so sorry."

She affected a smile. "It's alright," she said, leaning back a little too quickly. "I like the peace and quiet, anyways."

If Lucia had been looking through her before, she was boring into her, now. Agnete swallowed again. Her gaze felt like a hard reprimand. Agnete had been dismissive... evasively so. It was a reflex. But she wasn't a practised liar like Lucia was. She wasn't an actor. The words had felt clumsy and disingenuous even as they left her mouth.

"...I'm sorry," Agnete said when she recollected her nerve, "I'm not used to talking to people. *Really* talking. And not about myself. Usually, it's just business...

and sometimes listening to people unloading their own problems."

Something tugged at the corner of Lucia's mouth. "That must make for some excellent gossip."

"It would, if I had anyone to gossip with." Lucia gave her another thoughtful, piercing look. "...What?" Agnete asked after a moment.

"I don't think you would gossip," Lucia answered. "Even if you had someone. That's what makes you so easy to trust."

Agnete's cheeks coloured as she tried to figure out how to take the remark. *I've never really thought about it that way.* She certainly *liked* to think of herself as trustworthy. But it was an easy assumption to have about yourself when you didn't have many opportunities to put it into practice.

A small sigh left Lucia's nose. "This village doesn't know how lucky it is to have you."

Agnete felt as though a small egg had appeared in the back of her throat. She fought to keep her eyes from dampening, embarrassed. *No one has ever said that to me, before.*

Lucia had to have noticed; she straightened her spine and leaned gradually back into her chair. "So, then," she said lightly, "Speaking of family... Is my child to have any siblings? I'm not one to tell you how to parent, nor do I want to pressure you into making any big decisions... But I think I should like it if they did."

Agnete cleared her throat and answered as soon as she trusted herself to speak again. She certainly wasn't *opposed* to having more children...

As they kept talking, she couldn't help but notice something.

'*My child*', Lucia had said. *My* child.

It could have been nothing... A slip of the tongue, or meant in a strictly biological sense. But it didn't stop concern from embedding itself in the back of Agnete's mind.

7

Agnete could see the arch in Lucia's brow as she scurried over the threshold and through the door of her house, clasping her shawl tight around her shoulders. It was the exact thing that marked her as a witch, but she clung to it now as though it might make her invisible.

"Are you quite alright?" Lucia's blunt tone told Agnete that her husband was absent.

Agnete didn't know how to voice her worries in a way that didn't sound silly. "They've been... *seeing me.*"

"Of course everyone has *seen* you," Lucia answered dryly, "It's the middle of the day. Everyone knows who you are."

"It isn't just that. People have actually been saying *hello* to me. They've... never done that, before."

Lucia thought a moment "They've been watching you come here," she concluded. "That's to be expected. They're looking for gossip."

Agnete wrung the fringe of her shawl between her fingers. "Should I... come in through a back door?"

"No. No, of course not. Actually-" a slow, devious smile slinked across Lucia's face- "I have a better idea." She stepped over to the coat tree and pulled off a shawl embroidered with fine thread and tiny beads. "We're going out."

"Aren't we trying to *avoid* gossip? Or suspicion?"

"They're going to talk, regardless. What matters is *how much* they have to talk about." She set to tying a neat knot at the front of her shawl, her fingers improbably deft in their precision. "If they can't see our interactions, then they can make up all kinds of ridiculous stories about what's going on behind closed doors. But if they see us out together, smiling, laughing, being generally very friendly...

It'll be easy to believe that I'm just trying to make friends with the poor, lonely witch out in the woods."

A pity friend. Great. "So I'm a charity case?"

"Well, I wasn't going to be that indelicate, but..." When she saw the look on Agnete's face, she added, "There's no need to be upset. I'm the darling of the entire village. My reputation will rub off on you- before long, you'll have more friends than you know what to do with. Besides-" she turned and looked Agnete in the eye, one hand on the doorknob and the other on her arm- "*You and I* both know that you're not a charity case."

Agnete sighed as she opened the door. *I guess that's all that matters.*

-

"I think it's a little strange," Agnete said. "That I still haven't met your husband."

"He's a busy man. Or at least he fancies himself one."

They strolled leisurely through the streets, the smell of damp earth and smoke following them wherever they went. Lucia had very deliberately threaded her arm through Agnete's the minute they left her house, keeping them entwined as they walked.

The closer they wandered to the outskirts of the village, the easier it was for Lucia to ease out of her mask. Still, she spoke quietly, cautious of particularly ambitious eavesdroppers. "The less time I have to spend with him, the better." When Agnete didn't reply, Lucia turned her head to look at her. "What?"

"It just... makes me sad to see you so unhappy," Agnete admitted.

"...It's fine," Lucia replied, peering blankly into the trees. The green was almost entirely gone from them now. Shades of rust and scarlet were stark under an overcast sky, weeping fire onto the ground. "It's temporary. At least, that's what I tell myself."

Agnete swallowed. "If you ever need somewhere to stay... Or just somewhere to take a break from pretending..."

"It's okay," she said, shaking her head, "He isn't violent or anything like that. He just..." She exhaled, sharp and decisive. "He loves me. But he loves me as one loves a pretty doll. He loves to look upon my beauty. He loves to see me doing pretty things in his home. He loves how my attentions make him feel."

Agnete wasn't convinced. *That doesn't sound like love to me.* "Does he know a single true thing about you?"

It felt like a bold question to ask. *Too* bold. But Agnete was relieved and crestfallen when Lucia went quieter than she already was. "No," she answered, "I suppose not. I suppose no one does." She opened her mouth as if to say something before hesitating and closing it again. She licked her lips. "But I suppose there's something liberating in that."

Somehow, Agnete remained unconvinced.

"I'm sorry," Lucia said abruptly. "You probably feel the same way. Unknown. Unseen for who you are."

"...A little." *A lot.* She felt her arm go rigid around Lucia's. "It's silly, but... I talk to animals a lot." When the laugh didn't come, she confessed, "Honestly... I feel like they understand me better than people do."

"Animals as in... *forest* animals?"

"Yes... whoever comes by. Squirrels, chipmunks, birds, deer, foxes... Or any injured ones I find and take back home to help."

"Familiars?"

"No. That's just a myth. Witches don't have familiars."

"Maybe you should." Then, after pondering the idea, "I think I should like a familiar, if I were a witch."

"You don't have to be a witch to have a familiar."

"Sure you do. Otherwise, it's just a pet."

Agnete giggled. "What do you think familiars are supposed to be?"

Lucia shrugged. "They have to serve *some* purpose, in theory-"

"Like companionship? Or mousing? Or guarding? Or finding things-?"

"Alright." She playfully pushed against her. "Point taken."

"You know... I think you would make a good witch. In your own way."

"Why in the *world* would you think that?"

"People would seek you out for your skills. Not your beauty. And they would already fear you, simply *because* you're a witch."

"I don't know a thing about witchcraft, though."

"No. But you're great at reading people. You know how to tell them exactly what it is they want to hear. Or what *you* want them to hear. Which means that you can tell them what they *need* to hear, too. And that's usually far more valuable than any herbs or charms you can give them.

"Besides... you're so determined that you could study everything you need to know. Goddess knows you'd have the time. You'd probably be even better than me," she added with a self-deprecating laugh. "If you wanted to, you could probably fashion yourself the most powerful witch on this side of the mountains, with a little clever social engineering. With your ambition, you could create whatever reputation you wanted for yourself."

Lucia smiled. "It's a fun fantasy. I think you're selling yourself short, though."

"That's kind of you to say, but-"

"*Agnete.*"

Lucia had stopped abruptly, almost causing Agnete to stumble. Lucia's grip on her arm was as firm as her voice. Her breath hitched in her throat as she waited, wide-eyed, feeling as though something were growing thistles in her chest.

"I'm good at reading people. It's true. And I'm a good listener. But when I... *comfort*, or encourage, or advise, I do it for my own gain. When *you* do it, you do it because you genuinely care. That makes you more than just a good witch. That make you a good person. Truthfully..." she removed her hand from Agnete's arm and clasped her own wrist at her waist. "I think you're probably the best person I've ever met."

Agnete looked at the ground, trying to hide the colour blooming in her cheeks. Her fingers instinctively started fidgeting as she tried to recall how to form sentences. The weight of her own silence bore down on her with each passing second, a slow-swelling panic rising to meet it. She felt Lucia's arm cradle itself into hers again. The panic began to fade away as they continued their walk. Her silence didn't feel like such a failure, anymore.

-

Approaching the porch of Lucia's home, a middle-aged woman waved at them as they passed her on the street,

"Good day for a stroll," she offered. It wasn't, really.

"Yes, quite," Lucia responded pleasantly. "Enjoying the day yourself, I hope, Sofía?"

"Oh, well enough, well enough." She looked cautiously at Agnete. "I hadn't realized you were making house visits, Crona." Then to Lucia, "Nothing too serious, I hope?"

Lucia affected a soft, breezy titter. "Not at all! Not unless you count the want of a new friend serious, of course!" She turned and climbed the porch steps with a charming smile and an easy pace.

Agnete hesitated before following, a short pang blowing through her chest.

Right. The charity case.

8

"We would *love* four of your cinnamon cakes- Agnete simply *adored* them when she was over last!"

Agnete watched Lucia count coins into her palm. She had taken her to the baker's shop- the *cakes and sweetmeats* baker, not to be confused with the *bread* baker- and had promptly picked something familiar. It was for the best. If she hadn't, Agnete surely would have spent an uncomfortably long time eyeing everything on and behind the counter.

She passed the money into the baker's hand, only to feign mortification a moment later. "Oh, no," she exclaimed after having put her little embroidered purse away. "I've just noticed your sign, I've shortchanged you terribly! Please, allow me..." she trailed off, a calculated flush to her face as she began fumbling for her purse again.

The baker looked at her like she was a wounded bird. "Please, Lady Mayor, don't trouble yourself-"

"I insist, I couldn't possibly-"

"No, no, you haven't left me as wanting as all that," he said. "Here, take a pair on the house- for your *friend*." The word came out stiffly. He handed Agnete the cakes. "Crona."

Agnete couldn't tell whether the man really wanted to be generous, or if he had felt compelled to be. She wasn't entirely sure why Lucia had felt the need to do this in the first place. Maybe it was her way of treating Agnete. Maybe her disdain for the village and the people in it ran so deep that this was her way of lashing out.

"Oh, I'm so embarrassed-" Lucia pressed a hand to her cheek- "Truly, Marko, you're far too kind for someone who works themselves so weary." Lucia gave him a look which- if Agnete was being perfectly honest- probably would have melted her heart, too.

That wasn't the first time she had used that line. The first time she had phrased it that way, perhaps. But not the first time she'd expressed the sentiment to someone falling at her feet to give her preferential treatment. *"Everyone* is tired," she had told Agnete. "Give them a little recognition. Confirm the belief- *or the projection-* that they're working harder than everyone else, no matter how hard they're actually working. In a few words, you make them feel seen and appreciated in a way that, probably, only *you* have made them feel."

Agnete didn't like how much sense it made. *Feelings that aren't sincere shouldn't be allowed to make more sense than the ones that are.*

They were out strolling the streets of the village again, nodding at every passer-by they caught staring. Lucia had to maintain her mask. When they past a florist's stall, Agnete found herself unable to look away from a cluster of wine-hued Autumn violets. Lucia caught her looking- inevitably- and promptly bought her a small bouquet.

"For your cottage," she had said. But they ended up playing with some of the stems anyways, one of the dark little blooms ending up in Lucia's hair, tucked behind her ear.

"I must admit, I don't know *why* everyone insists on calling you 'Crona'," she said as they wandered down another row of tall, narrow houses covered in wooden shingles. "It seems a little... *dated,* don't you think?"

Agnete shrugged. "It's just the title people use to address witches."

"Oh, I know, but it conjures up an image of someone... decidedly older. It doesn't seem flattering for a lovely young woman like yourself."

Of all the parts of Lucia's mask that Agnete found objectionable, this might have been the worst: Not knowing if the good things she said about her were sincere or not. "What's wrong with that? I don't mind. Most of us grow old eventually. We get wiser and better at our craft. Why should that be a mark against anyone?"

"I don't mean to say that it should be... Only that it doesn't seem entirely fitting. There really should be an alternative title..."

"Like 'Lady Mayor' or 'Mistress of the House'?"

Lucia gasped with delight. "Yes, precisely! You could be 'Lady Healer' or 'Mistress of the Woods!'"

Agnete smiled despite herself. "Yes, those are just as short and unpretentious as 'Crona'."

"Well, *I* like them," Lucia rebutted. "I'll never be able to think of you as a haggard, wizened crone."

There it was: another compliment given under guise. It made Agnete want to push her luck, just a little bit.

"Come, Lucia, you know that if you want something, you can just ask. You don't need to resort to flattery."

The barb wasn't very sharp, but it prodded right where she meant it to. The flash of steel in her eyes disappeared as quickly as it came. "Agnete, you're positively *terrible!* You wound me!" She made a playful lunge at the cakes in Agnete's hand. "I ought to take these and eat them myself-!"

Agnete shrieked and pulled her hand away, shoving one of the cakes protectively in her mouth. She stumbled, noticing two seconds too late that Lucia had stopped.

When she turned and saw the three men standing in front of them, she hastened to recollect herself. Her fingers found her lips as she tried to chew away the large mouthful of food she had just taken.

Lucia glided over to the man on the left. "My darling!" She took his hands in her own and seemed to wonder at him, lovestruck and girlish. "It's such a pleasant surprise to see you during the day!" Bartrand was a man somewhere in his sixties. He seemed gratified as Lucia peppered him with questions about his day and whether he had eaten enough for lunch.

Agnete took the opportunity to steal a glance at the two men beside him: she recognized them easily enough. Emmerich was another member of the village council, mainly responsible for record-keeping and other administrative duties. At least, to Agnete's knowledge... She was more familiar with his wife and daughter, who periodically saw her for charms to ward away nightmares for the child. She had also supplied willow bark brushed with tincture for his son when he had broken his leg just over two years ago. She was less familiar with Friderik, the man standing in the middle of the trio. Early into his forties, Agnete knew that he was effectively the village's master of construction. His father before him had been the go-to builder in the village, spending his life teaching and directing other boys and men in construction- primarily homes and barns. His father was injured and rendered unable to work around twenty years ago now, leaving Friderik to fill his shoes before his twentieth year. Agnete remembered him visiting her mother perhaps once. He had never come to see her.

Lucia affected another abashed expression while her husband fiddled with the violet in her hair. "Please, forgive my rudeness-" she stepped back and turned to the other two men. "It's a pleasure to see you both again. I hope you've been doing well?" Emmerich responded with equal politeness, Friderik with a brusque affirmative. "I trust you both know Agnete?"

Emmerich nodded to her. "Of course, it's a pleasure to see you, Crona-"

"An unexpected pleasure," Friderik rumbled, a barely-detectable sneer directed at the violets in Agnete's arm. "Didn't think you ventured into town too much."

Agnete swallowed. "I do, of course... Just not too often. Generally, only to run the odd errand or make the rare house call."

"And which is it today?"

"Neither!" Lucia rested her hand on Agnete's arm. "She's simply indulging me, acting as my chaperone for the afternoon."

Bartrand spoke, then. "Very kind of you to ask her, my dear."

A needle ran between Agnete's ribs.

"Husband, you do see the best in me... But that's hardly true. The daily chores and strolls around town can get so tedious without someone for company. Agnete makes it *far* more enjoyable- she is so lovely to talk to, and knowledgeable about so many things, I'm just fortunate that she seems to find my company *half* as agreeable as I find hers!" Agnete struggled to keep the pleasant smile on her face as Lucia turned her saccharine attention towards her.

She felt Friderik turn his eyes to her- *had he ever taken them off?* "I guess it helps to have friends in high places, doesn't it?"

Lucia tilted her head. "I'm sure I don't know what you mean."

I'm sure that you do, Agnete thought.

It always seemed to be bad luck for a witch to merely *exist* in one's vicinity, until you needed their help.

Emmerich did the polite thing, trying to diffuse the undercurrent of his friend's remark. "I'm sure he didn't mean anything by it- Lady Mayor, Crona- just a little passing joke-"

"Tell me, Crona, is it good luck?" Friderik asked, "To count a witch as a friend?"

Agnete felt the cake in her hand start to break and squish in her fingers. "...I should think it good luck to have *anyone* as a friend," she answered carefully. "True friendship is a rare blessing to find-"

"I suppose for some. That's the thing with friends, isn't it? The more people you *talk to*, the less rare it becomes."

"I don't know about that-"

"I'm sure that's why the Lady Mayor has so many friends." A clump of crumbs fell onto Agnete's shoes. "She has a gentle nature. Hospitable. *Trusting.*"

"I'll thank you not to speak for me," Lucia replied in as much of a snap as she could get away with. "And forgive me, but I don't care for what you're insinuating. I hardly think you have any right, especially after your part in the rationing of firewood this year." He blanched as she looked to her husband- "I'm sorry, my love. I don't mean to be untoward, but I just can't *stand* to see your kind heart being taken advantage of-" and back to Friderik- "I haven't said anything because I haven't wanted to meddle- I *hate* to cause trouble, or make anyone think poorly of a man for trying to save his livelihood. But I won't stand quietly by while you're so needlessly rude to my dearest friend in all the world."

The men were all taken aback, and Agnete felt an unexpected pang of anger.

'My dearest friend in all the world'.

Something inside her hurt. It hit her fast and hard. The needle in her chest grew into a knife.

Lucia huffed, a delicate show of haughtiness. "I'm sorry, husband, I think I should return home... Please, love, don't let me sour the rest of your busy day. Agnete will see me back."

Agnete, still bewildered, allowed herself to be turned around and led away as Lucia linked her arm through her own.

"*Quickly,*" she whispered to her, all of the breeze gone from her voice, "*your half-eaten cake. You should turn around and offer it to him.*"

She understood exactly what Lucia was suggesting. *It's bad luck to reject a witch's hospitality.* If she offered Friderik her scraps and he rejected it, then according to superstition, he would be cursed. If he accepted it... he may as well get on the ground and kiss her shoes. Alternatively, considering what had just happened, it could easily be decided that she cursed the food as she offered it to him, as a way to punish him.

Either way, it was impossible for him to win. *The ultimate power move.*

Lucia had slowed her pace, giving Agnete ample time to act.

She thought. She fought back the prickly feeling under her eyes. She glanced over her shoulder, at the men starting to fold towards each other.

She said nothing and kept walking.

She couldn't tell whether it was because she believed it was the right thing to do, or because it was the only way she could think of in that moment to spite Lucia.

It was hard for Agnete to think over the hurt that week.

There was no one to talk to. No one to listen and make the hurt smaller. So instead of giving the hurt a place to breathe, Agnete spent the whole week warming it. *Proofing* it. Letting it grow into something that saddened her in a way she didn't know she could be saddened before.

When she stepped into Lucia's house again, she did so quietly. She didn't remove her shawl or shoes, but still told her, "I'd like to stay inside this week, if that's quite alright." She'd had enough of people staring at her on her way in; she hadn't needed to raise her eyes from the ground to feel their attentions on her. She felt as though she were walking through walls that were slowly closing in on her from every side.

"...As you wish." She could hear Lucia's furrowed brow. "I'll go put on the tea-"

"You don't need to."

Lucia wasted no time. She plopped her shawl and her coin purse on a small table and put her hands on her hips. "What's wrong?" When Agnete didn't immediately answer, she said, "If this is about what Friderik said last week, I can assure you, he hasn't *dared* to repeat it. Unless..." she started crossing the floor. "If he's so much as *coughed* in your direction, I will *personally-*"

"I'm not upset with Friderik."

"Then why are you upset?"

Agnete tried to answer the question. Except she didn't want to start at the beginning. She wanted to start in the middle, where they were already arguing and she was already armed with every thought she had cried over since their last visit.

She wasn't brave enough to start in the middle.

"I'm not going to play a guessing game," Lucia said. "Not with you. Don't pretend that nothing's wrong. It's plain that something is. So just tell me."

I can't do it. I'm a coward. Part of her hoped that, now that they were together again, it would be easier to forget and move on. "I don't want to talk about it."

"...You're angry with me, aren't you?"

"I told you, I'd rather not talk about it-"

"That's rather unfortunate, because I *would.*" She strode past Agnete and into the parlour. She wasn't running away. She was charging *towards.* But something in the sight of her back, of her walking away, pushed Agnete over an edge. "Go on. What have I done? I can't address what I don't-"

"Why did you have to say that about me?" Agnete demanded. "Why did you have to call me your *'dearest friend in all the world'?*"

Lucia faltered. "...Because-"

"Because you have a reputation to maintain? Because you wanted to make me look more desirable? So I can make my *own* friends? Which I *never* asked you to do for me, I'll remind you." She tried to stop her lip from quivering. "Maybe you just imagined yourself doing something generous for me. *Fine.* But you didn't have to be so *cruel* about it.

"You *know* that everyone is afraid of me. You *know* that I have no family or friends to speak of. We talked about it. I *trusted* you. I thought you understood. And your passing me off as your 'dearest friend in all the world', until you've had what you wanted from me, was cruel."

Lucia gaped at her. "I... still don't understand."

"We both know that's not true."

She swallowed. "I... I wasn't-"

"Listen to me... I *know* that this is just business for you. I'm not naïve. I know that I'm just another ingredient in your master plan. But-" her voice hitched and wavered. She wished the shadows of the house would consume her. "But you're the only person who *really* talks to me. You're the only person who actually spends time with me, even if it is all just for a ruse. It *hurt* when you said that I was your best friend. Because truthfully... you *are* my best friend." She smeared a sleeve across her face. "And it hurts to be reminded of how *pathetic* that is."

Agnete couldn't bring herself to look at Lucia for some time. When she didn't hear her dismissing her, or admonishing her for her sensitivity, she considered storming out. But the tension in the room held her legs in place like nails in the floor.

When she finally did risk a glance at Lucia, she was surprised to find her eyes avoidant and her arms trying to fold themselves back into her body. "...You thought I was lying," Lucia said. "I suppose I can't fault you for thinking that." She smoothed her hair back from her face with one restless palm. "You're the only person who's seen me as I am. You *know* me. You know the person I am around everyone else, and you *still* choose to spend time with me when I don't have to be that person. That Lucia is kinder and happier and more palatable. But you still only spend time with her when *I* ask you to." She inhaled. "You're the only person I know who doesn't expect anything of me.

"The best lies always involve a little truth... And I was telling the truth, when I said that. You're my best friend, too."

Agnete had never seen Lucia looking so uncomfortable. She brushed her sleeve over her cheek

53

again, using the edge of her shawl to dab at her chin. "You're not just saying that to make me feel better?"

"No," Lucia replied, punctuating the word with a quick sniff. "I think I even have you beat on the *pathetic* scale."

A small guffaw left Agnete's throat. "You aren't serious."

"You don't get the opportunity to make friends. I get dozens of opportunities every day, and yet my best friend is my drug peddler."

They looked at each other, cracked, and broke into a fit of giggles.

"Your *husband's* drug peddler." Agnete's correction elicited an extremely unfeminine snort from Lucia. They laughed harder.

Agnete couldn't tell how long it was before they managed to collect themselves. It had been long enough for both of them to collapse into chairs, too weary to support themselves any longer.

"I don't want to lie, anymore."

Lucia spread her hands. "Well..."

"About us. I don't want to be pretend friends. Or... pretend *real* friends. If everyone is to see us as friends... then I want to be true friends."

Lucia nodded, putting her hand over Agnete's. "Yes."

-

Agnete changed her mind about not leaving the house that afternoon.

Edging around the village square, Agnete noticed Friderik standing alone against a long cart, pointedly ignored by everyone around him. Lucia noticed her staring.

"Don't mind him," she told her, muttered near her ear to conceal the coldness in her voice. "He won't bother us."

"Is he alright?"

Lucia concealed a dagger-thin smirk. "He's had a rather difficult time making friends, lately. After word got out that he all but compelled my husband to impose the firewood rationing, no one's been particularly eager to commission his services."

"Firewood rationing?"

"I suppose you haven't heard... I'm not surprised. I don't imagine anyone would be willing to walk all the way into the woods to tell a witch that she can no longer take as much wood as she needs for her workings."

Lucia explained that for the last ten months, the entire village had been under a harsh wood and timber restriction; Every household, dependent on family size, was only permitted to cut and store so much wood. This had made it difficult for many homes, especially those with the elderly or the sick within their walls, to prepare food and sufficiently heat themselves. This was done, as per Friderik's recommendation, in order to "conserve limited resources". Of course, being the village's head of all construction, Friderik's business was exempt from the restriction. It seemed to make sense, since Friderik would have been the best judge of how necessary a structure was and whether it could reasonably be built with the resources at hand.

What the Mayor didn't realize was that many villagers had gone to Friderik for help when they didn't have enough firewood to get by. Friderik, more than happy to take advantage of the situation, had generously offered to help them by eating into his own building supplies to provide them with fuel. All he asked was a modest fee to "recoup a little of his losses".

"Suffice to say, either his reports of scarcity have been greatly exaggerated or his regard for said scarcity has been lacking. Either way... he doesn't seem so generous, now. I imagine he'll have a very difficult Winter ahead of him." She squeezed Agnete's arm and lifted her chin, self-satisfied. "That should teach him to be so disrespectful to such a valuable member of this community."

"If someone needs to be *taught* not to disrespect the Mayor's wife, I suspect they're beyond the point of learning-"

"Agnete, *really*." Lucia chuckled. "I meant *you*, sweetling."

Agnete's stomach fluttered again. She looked back to Friderik. "He doesn't have a wife or children, does he? A family?"

"No. He's alone."

10

Agnete was proud of herself for making it to Friderik's porch. She hated confrontation- which this wasn't, strictly speaking. But her stomach churned, anyways. She tugged at her shawl and tried to maintain her professional air.

He just stared at her when he opened the door.

"May I come in?"

He obliged, of course, lest some terrible misfortune befall him.

He shut the door behind her, leaving them alone together in the spacious, sparsely-furnished foyer. The rooms Agnete could see were mostly free of clutter, but covered in various layers of wear and wood shavings. She could see fine clouds of dust floating in the light filtering in from the windows. Odd splinters and curls of wood lay forgotten on the floor along the baseboards, congregating in the corners. There wasn't a sign of life in sight, apart from the two of them; no flowers, greenery, or baskets of fruit or vegetables. Just wooden floors, walls, furniture... impeccably smoothed and artfully carved. Beautiful wood that used to belong to something alive.

His home just made her feel more uncomfortable.

"I would like to request your services."

He stood stiffly with his hands hovering in his pockets, awkwardly half-submerged. His attention flashed towards the kitchen. He almost stammered. "...Did you want-"

"That's alright. I won't be here long." She didn't realize how hard she was gripping the bag of coins until she felt her fingers blanching. "I need a structure built. A barn."

"...A barn?"

He's skeptical. "There are a lot of animals around my home. Sometimes I find them sick or injured. It's easier to nurse them back to health if they aren't wreaking havoc in my home. And I've been thinking about keeping goats," she added. "Or chickens. Perhaps both. I haven't decided." Technically, that was true. She had been considering actually *using* the barn for its traditional purpose, purely so she could justify asking Friderik to build it with something other than a guilty conscience. "And it has to have a palette. Or maybe a loft. So I have somewhere to sleep if an animal needs care through the night. If the payment will cover it." *Lucia wouldn't have rambled on like this.*

He squeezed the tip of his nose between his thumb and finger, sighing into the crook of his palm. He still wouldn't look at her. "That's not going to be a cheap project."

"I know. But it's something I've been putting off for a long time. Too long." An audacious lie. She held up the pouch of money. "I can pay."

"It's not that I'm trying to gouge you..." He spoke more quietly than he had a fortnight ago, as though raising his voice to its usual level might make the situation even more uncomfortable. "But with the time it's going to take to get all the materials out there, and the amount of wood you'll need for it-"

"I don't need anything too big."

He gave his head a small shake. "Still-"

She unfastened the cord on the pouch and let it fall half-open onto the nearest surface she could find, a half-empty hutch. The bag hit the wood with a metallic *crunch*, spewing out a small handful of coins.

The important thing was that it was enough to see a person safely through the hardest months of the year, if they had no other source of income. What Agnete would never admit was that it was the vast majority of all the money she had in the world.

I'm lucky. I'm mostly self-reliant. I'll probably be fine. I just have to be a bit stingy with myself.

"Will that be enough?" she asked.

He cleared his throat and shuffled back on his feet. He rubbed at his chin, answering through his hand. "I'll, um. Take half now. And half when it's done."

Agnete straightened her spine. *How does Lucia do this so easily?* "You can start whenever you're ready. Thank you. I'm sure you know where to find me."

11

Keeping secrets felt easy when it didn't feel like they were hiding anything.

Lucia still had to maintain her persona, which meant all conversation held in public had to veer on the superficial side. But everything else that could be seen or heard between them as they took their weekly stroll was genuine.

They perused the myriad of stalls lining the village square, all overflowing with various trinkets, goods, and foodstuffs. The sun cast a golden light over the wares and warmed their backs as they shopped. A new scent seemed to pull them along every passing minute: the subtle honey of beeswax candles, the warm amber or woody musk of a perfume, the green-and-dirt scent of produce fresh from the ground. Agnete hadn't taken the time to enjoy the stalls in years- not since before her mother died. She was embarrassed to admit how excited she was to discover what was new and what had stayed the same; it was a heady mix of nostalgia and novelty. Several times, she had become so absorbed that she hadn't realized that Lucia had been staring at her. She always looked away the second Agnete noticed, which left Agnete feeling sheepish. *How sheltered and naïve she must think me... I must look like a child.* It hadn't helped that Lucia was making gifts of everything she *really* pored over. Every time she tried to dissuade her, Lucia would simply wave her protests away.

"Don't be silly," she would say. "I want to."

When the clocktower bellowed above them, causing the congregation of birds above it to take flight, the two of them returned to Lucia's home. Lucia lit the wood in the fireplace and brewed the tea that Agnete brought. They shut the curtains for privacy, eager to seal themselves away in their plush little den. They sat on the floor of the drawing room, sharing a pot of tea and plates of snacks. The treasures of their shopping trip lay scattered around them, close enough at hand to be admired on a whim.

"You didn't need to buy all of this for me."

"Don't be silly," Lucia repeated. "It's tiresome, always being the one who's spoiled by others. I never get the chance to spoil someone else. I was happy to."

Agnete smiled. "This better not be your way of sweetening me up so I let you off the hook for your end of our arrangement."

"Please," Lucia scoffed. "Believe me, you're getting the child. Never you fret."

Agnete took a thoughtful bite of her tea sandwich. "Have you always known that you haven't wanted children?"

"That... isn't exactly it. I just know I'd be a terrible mother."

"Why do you think that?"

"Have you met me?" she asked. "I'm far too ambitious for that. I care far too much about my own goals."

"I don't think that really makes any difference." When Lucia didn't answer, she asked, "Do you dislike children?"

"I don't dislike them. I like them well enough. I just don't think I'm the best person to raise them. It requires a certain softness of character."

"But you wouldn't say that about a father, would you?" Lucia froze, the blue teacup halfway to her lips. She inclined her head. "Touché." She took a sip. "It's alright. I'd be too scared of ruining them, anyways."

"I suspect all parents feel that way."

"And they all ruin their children."

"Do you think *I'll* ruin my children?"

Lucia laughed. "I can't imagine it. Well... probably not."

" 'Probably not. '"

"I'm a realist."

"*Well*." Agnete feigned haughtiness. "I'm looking forward to it. Not right away. But one day."

"So if I'm with child in the next year, you won't be prepared and I'll be off the hook."

"No. You'll just have to hold onto them for me."

"What if I don't want to?"

"You're terrible."

"That's precisely what I've been trying to tell you, and yet you refuse to believe me!" Her finger courted the edge of the plate in front of her. "You're not scared of being a mother?"

"Of course I am. I'm terrified."

"And yet you still want to do it."

Agnete's shoulder rose and fell. "Being afraid just means that you care."

"*Ugh,* " Lucia groaned, her eyes and head rolling back in a melodramatic arc.

"Well... you trust me enough to give me your child. If you believe in me, I'm sure I'll be alright."

For a moment, Lucia's expression was unreadable. Then she affected a smirk into her teacup. "I'm just foisting my child upon you. So I can focus on becoming wealthy and successful."

"I don't know that I believe you."

The silence sated itself on the sounds of crackling wood in the fireplace and the somniferous ticking of the mantle clock.

Lucia tucked her feet to the side. "...I suppose I'll miss seeing what kind of person they become. What parts of me they take with them. Just out of curiosity."

"You know..." Agnete moved her tea from her lap to the floor beside her. "...We could always exchange letters. Over the years, I mean. Keep in touch. Or visit-"

"Let's not talk about this."

Agnete drew her knees into herself. *I can't push her on this.* She hoped she'd figure her out before their time ran out together. She pushed away the heavy feeling in her chest. *I don't believe you're as callous as you say you are. I can't.*

It might be easy for others to ignore those fleeting, indecipherable looks that would pass across Lucia's face. But not for Agnete. She found herself collecting every one, tucking them away in her mind for later. She'd lie in bed at night and probe her fading memory, looking for clues like she'd comb through a bush looking for hidden berries.

"So what does your perfect future look like?" she finally asked. "If everything went exactly how you wanted it to. If the world were perfect."

Lucia thought for a minute. "I'd be doing something *respected,*" she started. "I'd live very comfortably. Presumably, with plenty of money. I'd have the freedom to do as I like. I wouldn't have to pretend anymore- at least, not all the time. I'd have the freedom to be *with* whomever I liked... Ideally with someone I genuinely loved." She straightened. "Realistically, I could be a politician's wife, or depending on the circumstances, a wealthy man's widow-"

"You mentioned doing something respected," Agnete said, "When you get out of the village, I assume? What would you do?"

"Mm... well..." she chewed on the tip of her thumb. "I suppose realistically speaking-"

"No, no, no. No 'realistically'. Imagine that everything you've ever wanted falls into your lap. You don't have to pay a price for any of it. What would you want?"

"I don't see the point in *not* being realistic about it."

"Just try it! I want to know. What would you do? Or just what would life look like? It's okay not to dream of a particular job. That's just one part of life, not the sum of it."

Lucia didn't answer right away. Her eyes seemed to glaze over as she thought. There was something about the way she looked that Agnete hadn't seen before. *She almost looks... lost.*

The usual sharp, agile focus returned to her eyes. She affected a subtle chuckle. "Well, it certainly wouldn't be witchcraft." Her tone warmed. "I can't imagine how exhausting it must be sometimes, being a caretaker for an entire village."

A deflection. She answered honestly, anyways. "It can be."

For all of her drive and all of that desperation... I don't think she actually knows what it is that she wants beyond an escape.

That must be frightening.

-

She left Lucia two hours later with a full stomach and even fuller arms.

"Oh!" She felt the pouch of herbs crunch on her hip as she walked over the threshold. "I almost forgot-"

She had to put a few things on the porch to give herself access to her belt. She unfastened the pouch and handed it off to Lucia, who then had to help her pick up everything she had just put down... including another pair of books from Bartrand's library that she insisted Agnete would love.

"You know," she whispered as Agnete was about to leave, "You can come more than once a week, if you like... If you're not busy, of course. You don't have to bring anything. It can just be for a visit." Then, hesitantly, "I enjoy our time together."

Agnete had to restrain herself from skipping home.

Once as she was stepping off of Lucia's porch, and again as she was leaving the village, she had someone smile at her.

Actually smiling.

Lucia was right- the fondness they had for her seemed to be catching.

12

Unsurprisingly, Friderik hadn't been touched with the same tolerance Agnete fancied she saw in the other villagers.

She had expected him to drag his feet building the barn for her. She hadn't expected to see him a few short days after she had knocked on his door, riding back and forth with a cart of lumber, clay, and sand. She had tried to direct him to practical spots to stack everything, but he barely acknowledged her advice. When she grabbed her axe and tried to help him enlarge the clearing around her cottage, he waved her away, telling her that he could make enough space for the barn on his own.

To his credit, he *was* fast, despite working alone. Agnete felt awkward going about her business while he worked, so she tried to do what she could: she cleared away branches and stones, and raked aside the carpet of copper leaves that grew thicker each day. Friderik paid the area roughly as much regard as he paid her, moving and removing whatever seemed to suit him best.

The first day, he worked well into the evening. Agnete approached him shortly before the sky started to darken. He didn't bother to turn his head in her direction.

"You don't have to work so late, you know," she told him. "Please don't feel like you need to work long hours on my account. I'm not in any rush to have it built."

He wiped sweat from his forehead and continued digging a trench for the foundation. "I want to get this done. Get out of your way as soon as possible."

He left shortly after the last light of the sun washed out of the sky. He didn't say goodbye.

He came back every single day, and she watched him carefully as she went about her business. She rarely saw him rest. She saw him eat even less.

"...Have you eaten?" She asked at one point, after mustering her courage.

He paused before he continued his work. "I am alright, Crona."

She pursed her lips. When he didn't stop his work, she left him. Despite herself, she was concerned. But she couldn't directly offer him food or drink without invoking superstition.

It doesn't matter how untrue it is... If he believes *that he can't say no, then I can't offer him anything.*

Unless... I don't offer it?

It took her an entire day to think of a way to think of a loophole. When she did decide to make an attempt, she made sure to watch Friderik even more closely than usual, to confirm that he hadn't eaten a full meal.

She walked out of her cottage, plate in hand. It was so heavy with foodstuffs- bread, cheese, nuts, fruits, and sweets- that she had to carry it with two hands. She placed it on a weather-worn wooden table, straddled by two equally worn chairs and near a firepit that she rarely used. She had to put the plate down hard three times to get his attention.

"I'm just putting this here," she said. He stared at the plate. "I've decided I don't want it. So I'm getting rid of it." She wiped her palms against each other, trying too hard to look nonchalant. "I wash my hands of it." She started to back away as Friderik squinted. "It's not mine, anymore." She started to turn around, only to turn back towards him. "Maybe some squirrels will eat it. Or... a person." She winced at herself. "But it's not mine, anymore. It's abandoned, now. Anyone can take it. I don't care. It's not mine to give anymore."

She scurried back inside, hopeful.

When it grew dark and Friderik left, she stepped outside. The base of the barn was coming along beautifully... and the plate of food remained untouched.

Later that night, she stumbled across a trap Friderik had set a short way into the woods.

She stayed awake late into the night, walking through the trees with a lantern and quietly disabling every trap she could find.

13

"You hired him. To build you a barn."

Lucia's tone was blunt. But it cut Agnete nonetheless. "...Yes?" She hadn't intended her answer to sound like a question.

"After the way he spoke to you?"

"You said that *no one* has been speaking to him... You said that he might not make it through the Winter-"

"I said that he was in for a *difficult* Winter."

"I felt... bad," she replied apologetically.

"He dug himself into this hole. He's being snubbed for a reason."

"Because... you defended me."

"*No.* Because he decided to give himself a benefit that everyone *else* had to pay the price for. I just made that clear to everyone. He wouldn't have been in this mess if he didn't choose to put his business before other people's health and comfort."

Agnete nibbled the edge of her nail. "...Maybe," she replied. "But even *if* that's true-"

"It is."

"-That doesn't mean he deserves to freeze, himself. Or starve."

"Doesn't it?"

Agnete stared at her.

"...Seems fitting to me," Lucia shrugged. Agnete peered down at her knees. "Has he at least been tolerable?"

Tolerable. He's the one who seems to find me intolerable. "...He's been tolerable."

It felt as though Lucia were looking right through her again. "If he's been anything less than a perfect

69

gentleman to you," she threatened, "I will come out there myself and-"

"He's been *fine*. He's... barely spoken to me. I actually-" she swallowed- "I tried to give him dinner. He almost never stops to eat anything, even though he works until dark. But he wouldn't take it."

"Did he at least say thank you?"

"Well... he didn't take it, so..."

"Tell me he's at least been civil." Agnete hesitated. Lucia breathed in sharply through her nose. "Agnete, I *swear*-"

"I don't need you getting angry on my behalf," Agnete snapped.

"Don't you?" she countered. "When you won't get angry on your own behalf?"

I don't get to be angry, she thought. *Not when they're already afraid of me.*

"It just *infuriates* me," Lucia continued, "seeing how everyone treats you. You are *nothing* but kind to them. And they treat you like *this*."

"They're just superstitious."

"And that makes it okay?"

No. But it explains it. And I don't know the difference between the two.

"...Did they even mourn your mother, when she died?"

Agnete's eyes prickled. She averted her gaze, trying to avoid Lucia, and found the nightblush cutting. It had started growing more stems now, spindly things that reached out in every direction and spilled over the rim of the vase.

That's the tricky part, her mother had said. *You tend to everyone else's maladies and heartbreaks. But when you have your own, there's no one to tend to you.*

She had been sick for months before she died. Agnete had cared for her the entire time. She had been the one to feed her when she grew too weak to feed herself. She had been the one to hum her to sleep. She had lain with her as she took her last breath. She had dug her grave, wrapped her in a shroud, and buried her herself.

Not once had anyone come with food or flowers or words of comfort. Not once had anyone come to help return her to the earth. Not once had anyone come to pay their respects to the woman who spent the last decades of her life healing them.

She felt the warmth of Lucia's hand on hers. Her fingers wrapped around Agnete's fist. "*Please* tell me that you know you deserve better than this." Agnete wiped a tear from her eye. "Haven't you ever wondered if you were meant for more?"

A humourless laugh escaped her. "Not really." She swallowed, sniffing away the tears she kept pushed down. "We can't all be as steel-hearted as you."

Lucia reached up and brushed another of Agnete's tears away with her thumb, letting her hand rest on her cheek. "People like you need people like me to protect them."

Agnete sniffed again. A small laugh escaped her, dampened by the tears and the trembling in her chest.

"Promise me that you'll stand up for yourself. You should at *least* be given simple courtesy."

"...I'll try. If I need to."

Lucia smiled, still cradling her face. Agnete felt herself seep into the thick cushions of her chair.

14

Agnete did her best to coax Friderik into speaking to her. She said "hello". She asked him how he was. She made pithy remarks about the weather. She complimented his work as he made progress on the barn. Lucia suggested she ask him about livestock: *"If there's one reliable way to get a man to talk, it's to give them half a chance to explain something to you."* But all that got her was two sentences and a suggestion of someone else to speak to, instead.

After a few days, she'd decided that she'd had enough. She spent the morning baking and putting together a spread for tea that she was admittedly quite proud of.

After surreptitiously watching through the window to make sure that Friderik hadn't eaten, she gathered everything onto a large serving tray and brought it outside. She placed the food and tea service on the table, everything positioned impeccably. She left the tea and the still-warm bread steaming behind her as she walked close enough to get Friderik's attention. She stood and watched him until he relented and turned his face in her direction.

She felt guilty. But she couldn't control what he chose to believe. And she couldn't take another day of feeling like a ghost in her own home.

"Would you like to join me for lunch?"

He looked past her at the table, at the wooden board of warm bread, butter, and cheese, and the tiered plates of vegetable pie and foraged fruits. *You won't be cursed if you say no,* she almost added. *You won't be cursed if you eat it, either.* But a small, selfish part of her stopped the words in her throat.

He murmured a traditional *"I thank you, Crona,"* and grudgingly made his way to the table.

Agnete sat with him; she could tell that he wasn't happy about having to stop in the middle of his work. She poured their tea and started smearing a thick, fluffy slice of bread with butter. She started eating far more quickly than she normally would have in the presence of a guest. It was an intentional choice. *Just in case he thinks it's poisoned, or some such foolish thing.*

But Friderik was still hesitant to touch anything. His eyes darted between every piece of food before him, as though he were assessing each item for danger. His hands remained on his legs as he shifted in his seat and grimaced at the tea in his cup, squinting at the steam curling into the air above it.

It was too much for Agnete.

She let her fists drop onto the table, causing the silverware and china to clatter. Friderik started. "Why do you hate me?!"

He gaped at her, utterly unprepared.

"I have been *nothing* but polite to you. I've tried to offer you food and drink while you work. I've tried to *talk* to you. I've *tried* to give you work that will keep you warm and fed until the snow melts. I've *tried* to repair the damage that Lucia has done-" she chided herself; *It wasn't entirely her fault-* "I have tried *so hard.* I have been *nothing* but kind to you! Why do you hate me?!"

He shuffled his chair an inch farther from the table, visibly uncomfortable. "I... wouldn't say *hate*, Crona," he muttered.

Agnete waited for him to elaborate. He didn't. "Then what?" she asked. "What else do you call it when someone refuses to speak to you? Refuses to so much as look you in the eye?" *Refuses to treat you like a person.*

As if to illustrate her point, he cast his eyes indiscriminately down. "It's... nothing personal," he answered. "You have to understand. Witches have a certain kind of reputation-"

"*'Nothing Personal'?* Do you have any idea how it feels? To be an outcast until someone needs something from you?"

"Well... That's just the nature of business, isn't it? Only being approached when someone wants something."

She sputtered, flabbergasted. "No-"

"Listen... I don't know why you're singling *me* out. I'm not the only person in the world who keeps their guard up, especially around witches. Everyone just wants to be cautious. Don't lash out at me just because I'm the only one who happens to be here right now."

Here. Working for me. "...You're here because I-"

"Because you approached me. Because you wanted something from me. You see how it's come full circle, now?"

He still wouldn't meet her eyes. *Good.* She prayed that meant he couldn't see them beginning to glisten. "...If Lucia can see past all of your ridiculous superstitions and get to know me- and see that I'm a good person- then everyone else can, too."

He didn't respond. When Agnete worked up the nerve to peer over at him, she saw that he was chewing one side of his bottom lip.

"What?" she asked. "What is it, now? *Tell me.*"

"It's just... strange," he said slowly. "Everyone's just saying that it's... strange."

"What's strange?"

"Just that... of all the women in the village, it's queer that the two of you are such close friends."

"Why should it be?" she demanded. "Why should our friendship be so strange?"

She glared at him and waited for him to answer, feeling her throat thicken with hurt. He swallowed and shifted in his seat again, arms drawn into himself. Everything on the table in front of him sat untouched, cooling in the crisp air. She pushed her chair out and stormed back inside, slamming the door behind her.

In a matter of minutes, she heard him back at work.

His words crawled in her skull and burrowed into her brain. She hadn't been seeing as many people as she usually did for healing and charms. She had thought that it was just a coincidence. She thought that perhaps fewer people were getting sick this year- a good thing, even if it meant less coin or exchanges for her. She thought back to what Lucia had said about the wood rationing, and wondered if everyone had less to spend on witchcraft after having to spend their money on wood for their bedrooms and kitchens.

It never occurred to her that there was another reason for the decline in people coming to see her.

If she had been braver, she would have told him to leave. To go away and not come back. But she couldn't bring herself to do it. So she locked herself inside and cried.

15

It would have been difficult to hide her gloomy mood from other people. But hiding it from Lucia was *impossible*.

When she asked about Friderik, about how he was, about what he had done or said, Agnete only told her, "He didn't say anything that wasn't true."

Lucia frowned at her.

"No one trusts me."

"Still?" she asked, "Even after showing everyone that you're my friend?"

It's because *we're friends,* Agnete thought.

Lucia scowled. "Regardless... That doesn't give him the right to be rude. Not after the generosity you've shown him. Besides... He doesn't speak for everyone. Especially after the entire village giving him the cold shoulder."

"...Maybe."

"What exactly did he say?"

Agnete sighed. "I... don't really want to talk about it. Let's talk about something else."

-

The layout of the streets became more hodgepodge the farther they tangled from the village square. Like most settlements, the village slowly expanded over time. Nature, human disagreement, or the presence of older, less cleverly-placed buildings often meant that streets had to form awkward angles, sudden curves, or tight alleys to accommodate new homes or shops.

This was what made it easy for Agnete to stay out of sight as she overheard two people speculating in hushed tones on her way back to the woods.

"...But to what end?" One asked. "Why not Bartrand?"

"Perhaps it's just more subtle this way. Or perhaps the Lady Mayor is an easier target," replied the other.

Agnete's stomach sunk.

"That still doesn't answer the *why*."

"I don't know... I couldn't say. Unless the Lady Mayor really has just been receiving house calls."

"*Regular* house calls? Accepting little bags of *who-knows-what*?"

Agnete's heart skipped a beat. *Oh, no... someone saw me give her the herbs.*

"Could be a regular dose of medicine. Could be anything."

"A regular dose of medicine she needs? Or that she just *thinks* she needs?"

The implication sparked a flame in the core of Agnete's body. She charged around the corner without thinking. "*HEY.*" The two gossips spun towards her, eyes wide. She couldn't replicate Lucia's iciest tone, but she tried anyways. "The Lady Mayor's *health* is none of your business."

The first whisperer clenched her jaw. "Forgive us for being *concerned* about our friend, Crona-"

'Friend'. You're not her friends. You don't even know her. None of you know her. The audacity left an oily feeling in her mouth. She felt her nails digging into her palms as they clenched at her sides. She didn't like the feeling of anger, the slow rage that tightened her chest. She wanted it to stop. She wanted *them* to stop.

"You should be *ashamed* of yourselves," she said with a low growl. "Those *little bags* are filled with fertility herbs. The Mayor and the Lady are having difficulties conceiving a child. They're *very* distressed about it. But they hide it *very* well. So I'll thank you to keep it to yourselves and stop gossiping like *vultures* about other people's struggles."

16

Agnete almost fell out of her chair when she heard the knock at her door. The shock was tempered by relief-part of her was afraid that she'd see the end of the next week before she saw another visitor seeking her services. She scurried over to her shawl and threw it on before hastily stumbling to the door.

When she collected herself enough to open it, Lucia charged through.

"What the *fuck*, Agnete?!"

She blinked. "Wh-?"

"You told someone that you've been giving me *fertility herbs*?!"

She swallowed. A black hole started opening in her chest, pulling the rest of her inside it. She felt stupid. "I..."

"I told you. *'Tell no one.' 'Say nothing'*!"

"I'm sorry..." She took a step away, and then another. "Someone saw me giving you the pouch of herbs lately... I overheard... They were talking about it, and they were saying the *worst* things-"

"Like what?" Lucia asked. "That we're plotting to slaughter the whole village and sacrifice their souls for eternal night?"

"That's not funny."

"I'll say it isn't. What am I to do, if my husband learns of this?"

"Just... say you kept it from him because you didn't want to hurt his feelings-"

"And when he learns that everyone knew but him?" she pressed. "And what about me? If I'm in a situation where I need to remarry before I make it out? How desirable is a woman who may not be able to give her spouse children?"

In truth, Agnete had regretted the decision the day she had made it. After she had time to come home and calm down, she had been hounded by guilt. "I'm sorry... I didn't mean to make things harder for you..."

Lucia sighed, heavy and tired. "You didn't mean to. But you have."

"I couldn't stand the way they were talking about me... about *you*. I wanted them to shut up. I wanted them to feel guilty." *I wanted the shame to bring them to their knees. I wanted them to hurt.*

She hadn't ever wanted someone to hurt like that, before. The feeling scared her.

Now here she was, crushed by shame. Lucia was angry with her. *And she's not even wrong.* Looking at her hurt. *I've lost my best friend.*

"I can stop coming by, if you want," Agnete murmured. "I know I already said... Um. I know the damage is done. But... it would stop things from escalating."

Lucia watched her, hands gripping her hips. Agnete tried to blink back the tears that were catching up to her. She waited for Lucia to agree with her, to say that *yes, that would be for the best.* But the ire began fading from her face. She sighed again, defeated. "No," she said, crossing the floor and wrapping her arms around Agnete. "I couldn't bear that."

A tear rolled from the corner of Agnete's eye. She leaned into Lucia's shoulder, sliding her arms around her sides.

"I'll figure it out," Lucia continued. "I'll try to keep this hidden from Bartrand for as long as I can. If I play the repentant wife, desperately trying to make her husband happy, then maybe- if I'm lucky- I can buy myself some time."

Agnete sniffled. "I really am sorry," she said into Lucia's shoulder.

"I know." She ran her hand over Agnete's hair and gave her a gentle squeeze before starting to pull away. "I came all of this way just to reprimand you... How about some tea and cookies?"

A tiny choke burbled from Agnete. "I thought you didn't like sweets."

"Yes, well. Ever since I've had you around to help me eat the excess, I've been regaining my tolerance."

17

Lucia's ability to garner information without having people directly *tell her* the information was nothing short of astonishing.

The entire village had begin pulling away from them both. Everything Friderik had said- or implied- was right. Agnete had been seeing fewer and fewer visitors. Even after Friderik finished the barn and stopped coming over, she would go for an entire week at a time without seeing a single person at her cottage. When her and Lucia went out for their regular strolls, shawls wrapped tight about their shoulders to ward off the quickly deepening chill in the air, neighbours had grown less likely to greet them. Everyone was hesitant to be caught looking at them or getting too close to them.

Their reaction wasn't solely directed at Agnete; Lucia was no longer offered the same special treatment she received before. She no longer received discounts or small gifts simply for being pretty and sweet. Merchants and shopkeepers seemed especially reluctant when Agnete was standing next to her.

When Lucia told her that the village believed Agnete was bewitching her, Agnete felt sick. The fact that Agnete had confirmed that she was providing Lucia with medicine- regardless of what that medicine was actually *for*- only served to strengthen their beliefs.

"That's how she does it, you know. Puts her under a spell and keeps her there with those magic herbs. If they even are *herbs. There could be anything in those bags."*

Some days, Agnete tried to give people the benefit of the doubt. She chose hope, and she tried to respond to their chilliness with warmth and geniality. But it never got her anywhere. Other days, she just tried to keep her head down and make herself as small as she could.

Lucia, on the other hand, began chafing under their assumptions. She was no stranger to being cast as the helpless maiden. But this was different. This time, she couldn't twist the situation to her advantage. This time, she had no control over it.

Her façade began to crack as her anger grew. At first, no one seemed to notice- at least, no one other than Agnete. She knew Lucia for who she truly was. She could see what others couldn't. She could tell when her smile didn't come as readily, or when it looked tighter than it should. She heard it when flattery or courtesy left her mouth sounding higher or more forced than it usually did. And she began turning down more and more invitations from her alleged "friends".

It didn't help their cause. But Agnete didn't know what else they were supposed to do.

"You *must* allow us to host you for dinner," yet another "friend" said, hiding their prying under the guise of hospitality.

"Perhaps another time," Lucia had responded.

"I *insist!* You've been cooped up for far too long. We all miss spending time with you-"

"Yes," Lucia said just a little more sharply than she should, "I understand you've all be *terribly* worried about me. Good day." She took Agnete's arm and promptly swept them both away.

Later, sitting in Lucia's kitchen and sharing a pot of tea, Agnete couldn't shake away the feeling of guilt. *This is all my fault... All of it.*

"You know..." Agnete said cautiously, "You can still save yourself."

Lucia cocked a weary brow. *"'Save myself'?"*

"Stop seeing me. Tell them that you broke free of my 'spell'. I'd drop the sleeping herbs off somewhere inconspicuous. So no one would see us together, anymore." She thumbed at the handle of her cup. It felt too smooth, too curved, too delicate. "...End our friendship."

"*No.*" The edge in Lucia's voice made Agnete look up. Lucia was glaring, until her features softened again. She shook her head. Then a second time, more softly, "*No.*"

18

Agnete didn't realize, as she walked head-down through uneven streets and wary passers-by, that this would be the second to last time that she would ever visit the Lady Mayor's house.

Her relief at reaching the imposing home didn't last. As she climbed the steps and readied herself to knock, she paused. Something felt... *off.* There was something different in the air, now that she was here. She slowed her breathing, searching for the culprit.

Sound. Noises. Voices inside the house.

Someone is angry.

She looked around- the street was empty. She slipped off of the porch and around the side of the building, letting the voices guide her to a window.

"...are the wife of an elected official! A *figure of authority*!"

"I know, husband, I know, that's exactly *why* I tried so hard to be discreet-"

"What part of regular meetings with a *witch* is discreet?!"

"She truly *is* my friend-"

"*Receiving* things from her? Everyone looks up to you! *Admires* you! How could you have thought to keep it '*discreet'*?"

Something rotten grew roots and bloomed in Agnete's gut. *'If I'm lucky,'* Lucia had said.

She hasn't been lucky, she thought. *Neither of us have been lucky. Not for a while.*

Town gossip had caught up to Bartrand, and he was incensed. She could hear the pleading in Lucia's voice, the softness she kneaded into every word. But her efforts, determined as they were, weren't working. Bartrand was having none of it. He cut her off every time she spoke, rejecting the honey she tried to feed him.

"And what if they see?" Lucia asked. "They don't know what the nature of the exchange is, I could have be taking *anything* from her-"

"But you weren't! No, if nobody *knew* what she was giving you, we could have told them anything. But that's not the case, is it? They *know* that they're for fertility. Do you know how that makes me look?!"

"Darling- not once did I *ever* think that the fault was with you. I- I assumed it *had* to be a problem with me. That *my* body didn't want to carry a child-"

"But will everyone else make that assumption?" The acid momentarily fell from his voice. "My dear, *no one* could ever see any fault in you. If they are to assume anything, they will assume the fault lies with *me*."

Agnete collected her courage and inched closer to the window. She managed the barest peek inside, just catching the edge of their exchange. Lucia stepped forward and reached a gentle hand towards her husband. "I don't think that's true-"

"I don't need coddling!" Bartrand pushed her hand away. "Do you *know* how you've made me look?!"

"There is nothing wrong with struggling to have children, it's *so common-*"

"But that isn't even the problem, is it? You never told me. You left me *in the dark! Everyone* knew before I did! My own wife, and I was the last to know! You have made me look a fool!"

"I didn't want to give you cause to doubt yourself! Or to add more stress to your life, when you are already so burdened-"

"This will affect how people see me as a leader!"

A stiffness filled in Lucia's shoulders. It was miniscule- Bartrand probably wouldn't notice. Not in his agitation. But Agnete could see the subtleties in Lucia's stance. How her movements became just a little less fluid, the nuance in the faint straightening of her spine. *She's struggling to keep her patience.* "How could it-"

"People could use this against me! This is how politics works-"

"Many men- many *people* have difficulty conceiving children-"

"But not knowing what his wife is doing behind his back?!" Bartrand spat. "Do you understand how stupid you've made me look? How untrustworthy?!"

Here it came- the quivering lip, the tears summoned strategically to Lucia's doe eyes. *She's getting fed up and changing tactics.* "I never meant for anyone to learn of it," she replied, turning away as if to hide her tears. Agnete saw her run the heel of her hand over her cheek. "I never meant to hurt you-"

"But you did. You went behind my back and deceived me," he said to Lucia's back. "You've put my reputation- my *position*- in jeopardy!"

"I truly don't think-"

"*Oh?* And what do *you* know of business and politics?" he sniped. Agnete watched Lucia's eyes go dead as the rest of her body mimicked weeping. Her mask faded into a look somewhere between annoyance and disdain. "You've spent your whole life being taken care of. You've *never* had to concern yourself with how everyone sees you! You've never had to *work*. You've never had to *protect your livelihood*. You know *nothing* of how the world works! You know *nothing* of the damage you've caused us!"

Lucia's face remained frozen in a faraway glare, discordant with the pitiful way she whispered, "*...Husband...*"

Agnete heard the sound of something full of liquid being picked up from a table. "Be sparing with the wood," Bartrand replied coldly, "And pray that you have not left us cold and hungry this Winter."

She heard him turn and walk out of the room. Lucia stood there, seething and unmoving.

Agnete started to panic when, after a long pause, she still hadn't moved or made a sound. Then, so abruptly it made Agnete jump, she spun around and pushed a thick armchair to the floor. It fell to the carpet with a muffled *thump* as she stalked rapidly back and forth like a caged tiger. Her hands balled into fists and formed grotesque claws by turn. She raked at the air around her chest and head. She twisted and grabbed several pillows from the furniture, whipping them around the room and towards the floor. She snatched one last cushion from the floor and slammed it to her face. She crumpled to the floor as she screamed into the fabric, the serrated, animal sound muted by jacquard and stuffing.

Agnete shrunk back from the pane as Lucia rose. The cushion fell to the floor beside her. When she turned away, Agnete had only a split second to see the tears smeared on her skin.

Fresh tears.

Real tears.

19

The last time Agnete ever went to the Mayor's home was in the dead of night.

She hadn't bothered with her shawl. She hadn't bothered with a lantern or candles to light the way there and back. She carried nothing with her but her entire supply of finely-ground psyllata root.

It was an easy task to slip around to the back of the house. There wasn't a single soul outside to sneak around on her way to the Mayor's kitchen.

Agnete tried the back door. As she expected, it was locked. She recalled a recent visit- she and Lucia had been sitting in the kitchen again, and Lucia had risen to shut the window some six, seven feet from the door. *'I open it to let the heat out, then forget to shut it,'* she had said. *'It doesn't want to stay in the track.'* It wasn't the first time she had mentioned the broken window.

The pads of Agnete's fingers felt around the edges of the window. With some cautious pressure, she was able to push the bottom just out of the track. She jiggled her fingers underneath and pulled, her breath catching as the old panes complained at being misaligned and lifted. She waited for any noise or sign of movement from inside. When none came, she pulled again, more carefully this time. The window slid up haltingly, starting and stopping every inch of the way.

Finally, Agnete figured that there was enough space for her to slip through. She put her hands on the sill, held her breath, and pushed off with her foot. She managed to get herself through the window up to her shoulders. With a restrained groan, she squeezed her eyes shut and pushed into her wrists, lifting her chest through. Her waist hit the sill, and she stretched her arms out into the darkness. She braced herself against the wall and shimmied herself further inside, biting her tongue.

Her heart skipped a beat when she felt her hips hit either side of the window frame.

She gasped. *"No... no, no, no-"* she tried again to squeeze through, only to feel the ledges bite harder into the meat of her sides. She swore under her breath and tried again- she could wiggle herself back out, but not further in.

She took a deep breath and started a count to three before trying again. *One... Two-*

"What are you doing?!"

Agnete's head whipped around at the hissed question. Lucia stood there in the dark, clad in a white nightgown. Agnete gaped at her- it took her a moment to remind herself to start breathing again. Lucia sighed sharply and stepped over to the door. Agnete backed out of the window as she unlocked it.

"What are you doing here?" Lucia asked again after Agnete was inside, door shut behind her. Agnete tried to answer her, but the words wouldn't come. She didn't know where to start. She reached into her belt and pulled out the sack of psyllata root, the size of a large man's hand. She fingered at the drawstring and opened her mouth to speak. Lucia took the bag from her and appraised it in the dark. When her fingers found the paper tag attached to the string, she looked back at Agnete. "What is this?" When Agnete hesitated, she sighed again and stepped into the hallway. Agnete heard the distant sound of a match being lit. In a moment, Lucia had returned, the warm glow of a candle casting shadows on their faces. She put the candle and the pouch down on the butcher's block, leaning on her elbows to squint at the tag. Agnete remembered what it said. *PSYLLATA ROOT. Strong Laxative. Three Pinches Dissolved in Liquid.*

"I came by earlier, when..." Agnete trailed off. "I heard how he spoke to you."

Lucia looked up at her. "...What were you doing with this?" she asked slowly.

Agnete swallowed. "I thought, maybe, if I put it where you hid the sleeping herbs, and came back to get it tomorrow..." she felt herself flushing. She started wringing her fingers. "Just for a day... Just for the morning, really. I thought you might want to add it to his morning tea..."

Lucia's expression was unreadable as she studied Agnete. Dread crept up the back of Agnete's skull as they looked at each other in silence.

Lucia started slowly shaking her head. "That's not how you do revenge," she breathed.

Agnete watched as she took her time walking from the butcher's block to a cabinet on the other side of the room. She opened the doors and pulled out a jar of sweetened fruit preserves.

"This is how you do revenge." She opened the jar and emptied a tiny pile of the pale powder into the jam. She reached into a nearby drawer, pulled out a small knife, and vigorously stirred the powder into the jam. When Agnete thought she was done, she watched her reseal the jar, only to reach back into the cabinet and pull out a partially-sliced loaf of bread.

"Won't you have to eat, too?" she asked as she watched Lucia dust the bread with the powder.

Lucia turned to her with a mockery of devotion. "I'm a good wife. I tend to my husband and bring him his meals when he's unwell," she replied. "I'll take my own meals if I have the time, once my husband has been well taken care of." She put the bread back in the cabinet and walked back over to Agnete. She put the bag on the surface between them, retrieved a block of butter and another knife, and pushed them across the block to Agnete.

Agnete eyed the butter, then looked back up at Lucia.

She picked up the bag and shook the powder into the butter.

They frantically rummaged through the kitchen, giggling and shushing each other. They put the psyllata root into a bag of oats, a half-empty sack of barley, a decanter of amber liquor, and onto a partially-eaten cake. Lucia pulled out a funnel and a heavy jar of oil; their fingers became coated in oil as they slipped the funnel over the jar and poured the powder in.

Lucia did her best to shake the bottle, glass slipping in her fingers. Agnete searched for something to clean her hands with, finding a drawer full of cloths across from the block.

"No no no, not those ones!" Lucia whisper-shouted at her when she pulled one out. *"Those are all decorative!"*

Agnete looked at the drawer, filled to the brim with neatly-folded cloths. *"All of them?!"*

"Just wait, I'll get you a-"

"Why do you have so many cloths that you can't even use?!"

"It's not my fault, they were wedding gifts!"

"Cloths are meant for cleaning! They're supposed to get dirty!"

"They were bad gifts. I don't even like them!"

A devious smile formed on Agnete's face. *"...I'm going to use it."* She inched the cloth closer to her fingers.

"NO-" Lucia lunged across the room at her. Agnete dodged, holding the cloth threateningly close to her oil-slicked hand. *"Give it back!"*

She sprinted around the room as Lucia chased after her. They both stifled a squeal when she finally caught up to her, grasping Agnete's arm and reaching as she held the cloth aloft. In her efforts to recapture the cloth, Lucia unwittingly smeared a soiled hand up the length of Agnete's sleeve. Agnete inhaled sharply in shock. Lucia's hands flew to her face when she realized what she had done.

Her jaw falling open, Agnete reached out and wiped her palm deliberately across the front of Lucia's nightgown, staining the light fabric with oil.

Agnete stumbled backwards as Lucia advanced again, only to find herself hitting a counter. She put her hands up defensively as Lucia's hands flew at her, her fingers sliding over the side of Agnete's nose in retaliation. Agnete tried to grapple her wrists, the oil sitting thick on their skin and making it impossible. In the scuffle, her fingers managed to find Lucia's cheek.

"You almost got that in my eye!" Lucia said as she wiped at the oil with her wrist.

"Stop, you're making it worse-"

"I can't see it-"

"Here, stop-"

"It's on my face!"

"Just let me get it!" Agnete firmly guided Lucia's arm away from her face. She lifted the corner of the cloth, letting it hover over the apple of Lucia's cheek. She put a guiding thumb on the curve of Lucia's jaw. *"Here, turn towards the candle, it's too dark..."*

She leaned in closer to inspect the shine on her skin. She cleaned the oil from her face, running the cloth over her cheek in small, gentle arches. When she pulled the cloth away to examine her work, she realized too late that her other hand was still lingering on Lucia's face, fingers pressed into her neck and the crook under her jaw.

Lucia had realized it, too.

She wanted to apologize, to pull away. But she froze. Lucia's skin was warm. She could feel her heartbeat pulsing against her fingers, quickening under her touch. They were too close. She could feel the ghost of her breath whisper past, their exhales measuring the space in something headier than seconds.

Agnete watched Lucia.

Lucia watched her, lips parted.

Her hand inched painstakingly towards Lucia's chin.

"Lucia?!"

They both jumped out of their skin at the sound of Bertrand's voice booming from upstairs.

Lucia squeezed her eyes shut and took a shaking breath. "I couldn't sleep," she replied, projecting her voice. "I'm just making some tea."

Agnete tried to concentrate on the feeling of the cloth as she squeezed it between all of her fingers. She shuffled backwards, gulping.

Lucia scratched the back of her neck. *"You should go,"* she whispered, *"before he gets suspicious."*

Agnete nodded and handed her the soiled cloth. As Lucia started putting the laced foodstuffs away, Agnete made her way back to the pouch. She picked it up- it was significantly lighter than before. Before she could close it, Lucia stopped her hands. She retrieved a small glass and scooped an extra little mound of the powder inside.

Agnete closed the pouch and put it back into her belt as Lucia hid the glass in the back corner of a full cabinet.

"I missed seeing you today," Lucia said as Agnete stepped back out the kitchen door.

"Me, too."

Lucia leaned on the edge of the door. "Let's start meeting at night. After Bartrand and the rest of the village is asleep. I'll sneak out and meet you at home."

"There are animals in the woods," Agnete said, shaking her head. "I'm more familiar with them. And they're more familiar with me. I can walk you."

"That's alright. I'll stay on the path. I'll be okay."

They reached for each other's hands and gave one another a parting squeeze.

"I'll keep the hearth lit for you."

20

"You're eating more of those than I am."

"I can't help it. They're good." Lucia licked caramelized crumbs off of her thumb. "Here I was thinking nuts were just needless filler."

"No, they have their own flavours. You can make anything with them."

"So I've come to learn." She reached for another sandwich cookie.

There was something unspeakably rewarding about watching someone so dear to her fill their face with sweets that she took the time to make. Feeding others was a simple joy that Agnete hadn't experienced before. Watching someone else take pleasure in something she had put love and care into made her feel as though she were sitting in sunshine, despite the velvet black hour.

She smiled. "That was one of my mother's recipes."

Lucia finished chewing. "I don't remember your mother very well."

"I suppose you wouldn't."

"She was important to you, though." Lucia leaned forward and leaned her chin on her hand. "You talk about her a lot."

Agnete found herself wondering every day lately if her mother would have liked Lucia. She liked to believe that she would have. "Yes."

"After she died... Did you bury her nearby?"

"Yes... She's somewhere nice. Quiet. I made a little garden for her."

"Do you visit often?"

"A couple times a week." *More, now that no one comes to ask for my help.* "I tend to the flowers... And talk to her." She leaned into her elbows, planted on the table, and hid her mouth behind her fist. "You probably think that's silly."

"Not at all," Lucia soothed. "What kind of flowers did you plant?"

Agnete chewed the inside of her lip. In her mind, Lucia had already been with her at her mother's resting place. She had already imagined the words they might share. She had already tried to picture the way Lucia's smile would look in the dappled light, and attempted to calculate how her voice might swim in the whisper of the leaves. Her stomach buzzed. "...I could show you?"

A smile bowed Lucia's lips. "I'd like that."

-

The familiar scent of honeysuckle greeted the two women as they found the small clearing. Wildflowers grew long and untamed at the edge of the space, springing up around the base of trees and bending stems over their roots. Alyssum spread in a crescent-moon shape, stretching out from a stone squirrel statue- her mother had loved that weather-worn thing. She would jokingly call it her "familiar". Cornflowers, calendula, and poppies poked their heads out from the arc, awaiting the return on the sun. Columbines leaned in wayward directions, petals already falling off and decorating the ground with sparse confetti. The lantern light illuminated the honeysuckle vines climbing up the trunks of the trees, hanging from the branches, and spreading onto the earth below. It spilled shadows between the berries and the leaves, stretching the vines until they were deep enough to fall into.

Agnete fought to keep herself from openly looking to Lucia.

"This is beautiful," she heard her breathe beside her.

"Thank you."

"Your mom would have been proud."

"Yeah," Agnete sighed. "She always was."

Lucia stepped closer to her. "Tell me about her?"

Agnete tittered, suddenly nervous. "...She was good," she said. "She was kind. Warm. She made me cinnamon rolls when I was sad. She brushed my hair, even after I grew too old for it. She always kept too many candles and lanterns in the house, just in case anyone needed them to get home. She always made me take some candles with me whenever I left, no matter what time of day it was. Just in case. I still have a ridiculous amount of candles all over the house, from before she died." She laughed. "And for someone who lived in the forest... she was *really* scared of the animals. Not the small ones, I mean. She let the little ones into the house all the time. It's the bigger ones that made her nervous. I brought home an injured badger one day- I found it while I was playing. It wasn't even an adult, I don't think... just a little thing, really. I just wanted to help it feel better. And she *screamed* when I took it in the house. The second she saw it, she just *screamed.*"

Lucia glanced at the stone statue. "I imagine she was a good witch."

"She was... I think it took a toll on her, though. Being the only witch around for an entire village. Even a small one like this. *And* raising a daughter by herself... especially one as inquisitive as I was. Especially with how they treated her.

"I'd find her crying, sometimes. When things got to be too much. There aren't many places to hide from a small, curious child here. I'd crawl into her lap when I was little... I'd put my little arms around her and tell her *it was okay, don't cry.*" She swallowed. "I had to spend years telling her it was okay."

She felt Lucia's hand slip over her own. "I'm so sorry."

Agnete just nodded in response, clearing her throat. "I think it was hard for her. I know it was."

"No, I didn't mean her... although, I am sorry for her. I meant you."

She shook her head. "I was just a child. I missed a lot of it."

"Exactly... you were just a child." Her lantern swayed as she shifted from one foot to another. "You shouldn't have had to tell her it was okay."

"She took on so much... I don't think it could have been helped. She always put everyone else first."

"Maybe she shouldn't have."

A petal fell from somewhere above them, caressing Agnete's cheek and shoulder in its descent. She sniffed and passed a finger just below her eye. "Maybe... But she was still a good mom. A *really* good mom."

They settled into a few wordless minutes, crickets chirping in the dark around them.

"...Is it possible," Lucia eventually asked, "That your father was someone in the village?"

"I don't think so," Agnete replied. "She talked about other places, from before I was born... I think she settled down here to raise me." *And look at how it turned out for her.* The pang of guilt that followed was well known to her, now.

Lucia rested her head on Agnete's shoulder. "Well, I'm glad she did."

21

"I swear to you, she called me- her *exact words*- an 'innocent little lamb'."

Agnete snorted from her spot on the floor. Lucia was lounging on her bed beside her, twisting an impressively large leaf, picked up from the night's walk, idly in her fingers. The book that she had brought with her lay next to her, forgotten in favour of the day's gossip.

It was always the day's stories, now. Never the week's stories. Lucia had started traversing the woods every night, staying until the small hours of the morning with Agnete. It was taking a toll on both of them- the lack of sleep dulled their reflexes and painted dark crescents under their eyes. Agnete struggled to concentrate and found herself forgetting things during the day. *At least I'm able to sleep when I need to,* she often reminded herself. *Lucia has a large home and a husband to look after during the day.*

"Of course," Lucia continued, "I don't suppose she would have said that to my face. But still. A *lamb.*" She bounced up onto her backside and crossed her legs. "I should have said something. Let her know I heard her. That would have showed her."

"Aren't you trying to keep the *Village Darling* act going?"

Lucia shrugged. "I suppose... for now. But every day there seems to be less and less reason to."

Agnete sighed, leaning against the leg of her bed. *A little lamb. That* is *ridiculous.* "I think you're more of a fox."

"A fox?"

"Mm. Red ones, in particular."

"Why is that?"

Truthfully, Lucia did remind her of a fox. A specific fox, even. Shortly after Agnete's mother died, she came upon a fox who had evidently escaped from a trap- likely a villager who wanted to catch an animal for dinner or fur. The fox was badly hurt- her leg was matted with dirt and blood. Agnete spent long weeks nursing her back to health, only for her to depart suddenly one day, still limping. It had been surprisingly easy, guiding the fox back to her cottage. *She fought so hard to get out of that trap... and when she finally escaped, she didn't even know where she wanted to go.*

"Foxes are beautiful," Agnete answered, "and clever. They're *unbelievably* clever. They're solitary. And they're amazing hunters." *They also mate for life.*

But she wasn't going to say that out loud.

Lucia grew quiet and seemed to consider the idea as she leaned backwards against the wall. Agnete turned her head and looked across the room, to the fire crackling quietly in the hearth. Lucia's cloak and boots were left discarded in no particular order in the general vicinity of the door. Two mugs, one with a knitted sleeve, and an almost-empty teapot had been left where they were last used, between the chairs near the fire. A handful of plates and saucers lay scattered near the wash basin- a task for tomorrow. Miscellaneous books sat in random spots throughout the cottage, some half-read and other still forgotten by Lucia on her way out the door. The air was filled with butter and sugar, spices and herbs. Agnete had already pulled a couple of pillows from the bed to better cushion her casual spot on the floor. If she leaned to the side and rested her head on the mattress, she suspected that she could have fallen asleep, with Lucia right there above her.

"If I die, I'll come back to haunt you as a fox."

Agnete's eyes shot open. She choked and fell into an incredulous laugh. "Why would you say something so morbid?!"

"What? You never think about dying and coming back to haunt people?"

"No?!"

"It's a normal thing to think about! Everyone does it!"

"I don't think they do..."

Lucia rolled onto her side to face her. "If I die before you do," she said, "then I'll come back as a red fox. I'll get to see you as a little old lady. Maybe I'll even get to see how my child turned out, if they're still here. Or if they visit you. If they turn out to be awful, and you did a bad job raising them, I can bite you."

"And how would I know that it's you and not some random fox?" Agnete asked. "You're going to give me a fear of foxes!"

"You'll know it's me," she replied. "I'll wait with your mother. I'll meet you under the honeysuckle. I'll take naps there, right in the middle of your flowers."

Agnete swatted at her arm. "You're going to ruin my garden!"

"Your garden will be *fine*!" Lucia scoffed. "I'll even protect it for you. I'll eat all of the birds that try to pick at the honeysuckle berries."

"The berries are literally there *for the birds to eat.*"

"Not while I'm guarding them, they're not."

"And if you die after I do?"

Lucia thought for a moment. "Then we'll both have to come back as foxes."

"We can run around and play in the forest together."

"And bite people."

Agnete cackled. "You sound like a very mean fox. You sound like a *menace*."

"Hey! I spend every day of my life *not* biting people who deserve it." Agnete held her stomach and sunk deeper into the floor. "In fact, I spend every day being *nice* to people who, truth be told, I *should* be biting. Fox or not. I deserve this. Let me have it."

It took Agnete a minute to recollect herself. She hesitated. "Or... You could just visit while you're alive?"

Lucia sighed. "Are you planning on leaving this place?"

She chewed her lip. "I'm the only witch they have..." she said. It sounded weaker out loud than it had in her head. "And my mother is here..."

A look of regret passed over Lucia's face. "I understand," she said. She rolled onto her back. "...I don't want to come back."

"Not even to visit?"

She looked at Agnete. "You could visit," she countered. When Agnete opened her mouth to speak, she added, "If the whole village can go this long without you, then surely you can leave them for a little while?"

It was true; for the first time in her life, Agnete hadn't seen anyone in weeks. She had used most of her money paying for the modest barn outside. She had been starting to worry about Winter. She couldn't receive coin, goods, or exchange services if no one sought her help.

But what if she was needed? What if, while she was gone, someone's life depended on her aid? What if someone died because she wasn't there to save them?

She didn't know how she could live with herself if that happened.

"Just think about it," Lucia said. Agnete nodded. It felt dishonest. "If all else fails…" Lucia extended her little finger towards her. "Foxes?"

Agnete reached up and curled her little finger around Lucia's. "Foxes."

-

Agnete's eyes fluttered open. She hadn't realized that she had dozed off.

The windows still showed a night-blacked sky behind the reflections of her home. There was still a low fire burning in the hearth. *Good… I haven't been out for long.*

She lifted her head; Lucia was still lying on her bed, arm curled under one of her pillows. She was fast asleep, leaf still tucked under her fingers.

Every cautious part of Agnete told her that she should wake her. But it was impossible not to take pity on her. *She barely gets any sleep, now,* she thought. *She would rather spend time with me than get a single good night's sleep.* Her heart swelled into her throat as she watched her, peacefully unconscious. *Let her sleep… just a little bit. Just before she leaves.*

She brushed a spindly lock of hair from Lucia's face. It was a comfort and a novelty, seeing her asleep. The energy that seemed to pull others towards her had dissipated. Her eyes, always watching and responding in kind, were curtained. All that was left was a young woman, as still and small as Agnete had ever seen her.

She had tried to name everything that she had felt over the last few months. She came up with half as many answers as she did questions.

Lucia made her feel protected. For all of her own attempts at caring for Lucia where she could- feeding her, giving her a place to breathe, trying to make her feel at home- Lucia was the one who made her feel taken care of. The stares and suspicion of everyone else felt smaller when they were together. *'People like you need people like me to protect them.'*

It scared Agnete, how quickly Lucia had become her safe place.

She could have been happy, spending their days together. Even spending them here. But she knew that Lucia didn't share that feeling. Lucia was bigger. Lucia was *more*. Lucia had so much potential that she was wilting here. *Shrinking.* She still didn't completely understand why Lucia couldn't just take a cart and leave... But it hurt seeing her so confined. *She has so much potential. It's explosive. She could light the world on fire, if only she knew what it was that she wanted to burn.*

She nudged herself closer to the edge of the bed and leaned her head against Lucia's arm. She tried to tell herself for the hundredth time that *at least I'll get to raise her child. At least I'll get to keep a part of her with me.* But for the hundredth time, it wasn't enough. The idea of the child brought a deep, warm joy to her heart. But it was muted by the thought that Lucia wouldn't be there to share it with her.

She nuzzled as lightly as she could against Lucia's arm, careful not to wake her, yet.

She wouldn't be selfish. She couldn't be.

-

Agnete awoke to the scuffle of feet on her floor and whispered, panic-stricken curses. Her eyes adjusted to the light- the sun had risen outside.

Shit.

"Fuck fuck fuck-" Lucia whirled through the room, pulling on her boots, laces slipping through her clumsy fingers. She gave Agnete an apologetic look when she realized that she was awake. "I fell asleep," she panted, "I need to go-"

Agnete pushed herself up. Lucia whipped on her cloak. "I'm sorry-"

"It's not your fault-" she strode over to Agnete and brushed her cheek- "I should have been more careful."

Agnete followed her to the door. "What will you tell Bartrand?"

"I'll think of something on the way back-" she opened the front door- "I'm so sorry to leave you like this-"

"No, go, go-"

Agnete watched as she ran out the door and into the woods, her cloak billowing as the trees embraced her.

22

Lucia did not come back the following night.

Agnete was worried, but she tried to reason away her anxiety. *She probably just needed to smooth things over with Bartrand. She probably just needed to play the penitent wife for a little while. She probably has a plan. She'll probably be here tomorrow. I'll probably see her again, soon.*

Probably.

Probably.

She told herself the same things the next night as she waited for Lucia, hearth aglow and teacakes on the table. And the next. And the next.

Probably.

The word beat in her chest where her heart should be. *Lucia can take care of herself.*

Probably.

She waited days. And then an entire week. She spent every waking hour thinking about going into town to look for her. Fear of the unknown- and of her peers- kept her at bay. *If they've done something to their sweet, perfect Lucia... What would they do to me?*

Her fear made her feel weak. It made her hate herself.

When Lucia finally did appear before her, the sight of her made Agnete's heart stop.

It was the middle of the day. Agnete was tending her vegetable garden when she heard the furious crackle of something running over the leaf-laden ground.

Lucia appeared from between the trees, undone and breathless. She wore no cloak- only a simple dress and a pair of hastily-tied boots. Her hair fanned wild behind her as she sprinted towards Agnete.

Agnete shot to her feet, catching Lucia before she could accidentally shoot past her. "What happened? Are you alright?"

"He knows," she gasped, trying to catch her breath. Agnete took off her cloak and pulled it over Lucia's shoulders. She could feel her heart clanging against her ribs. "Bartrand knows."

"What does he know?"

"Everything. He knows everything- almost. He knows I-" she swallowed, nearly choking herself. "He knows how close we are."

Am I... missing something? "Doesn't everyone?"

"He knows that everyone believes that you've bewitched me. And he knows that I've been sneaking out at night to see you."

Agnete's mind clambered to put the pieces together. She recalled the way he spoke to Lucia, the day she overheard them at the window. *'You've made a fool of me,'* he had said. *'You've put my reputation- my position- in jeopardy.' 'You've spent your whole life being taken care of. You've never had to concern yourself with how everyone sees you.'*

Bartrand was a man who prioritized his position. He was a man who cared about how he looked... or how he *thought* he looked. He was proud. If he believed that he was the last to know the rumours going around about his own wife- the last to know about her sneaking around behind his back- he would be humiliated. He would be *furious*.

Lucia had been gone a week. And here, she was, running as fast as she could back to Agnete without so much as a shawl to keep the chill off.

If he comes for her, he will have to go through me, first.

Agnete cupped Lucia's face in her hands. "Do you need somewhere to stay?"

A look of confusion passed over Lucia's face. "What? I-" Agnete's meaning dawned on her. "Oh. No... no, I'm fine-"

"I can protect you-"

"No- I'm more worried about you." Agnete opened her mouth to ask what she meant, but Lucia was a step ahead of her. "Listen to me... He's been keeping me close for days. I haven't been able to get away. He's told me that it's for my own good. He's forbidden me from seeing you. He won't give me any opportunity to be alone."

"How did you get away?"

"He kept me close, but not necessarily within view. I mixed his sleeping herbs with the psyllata root and put it into every liquid in the house," she answered. "He can't drink anything without sleeping or shitting." She thought for a second. "Possibly both..."

"But why are you worried about me?"

"He's a powerful man here, Agnete... How long until he convinces everyone to come here with torches and pitchforks? He hasn't said anything to anyone, yet... He's still stewing in his embarrassment. But for how much longer?"

Agnete suddenly felt cold. *I've eased their pains and healed their children. I've helped them feel lighter when their lives became heavy. They couldn't. They wouldn't.*

And yet... the dirty looks when they thought she couldn't see, the distance they kept from her, the gossip, the rumours, the assumptions, the belief that the only way she and Lucia could *possibly* be friends is if Agnete was manipulating her...

And yet.

She knew what Lucia would probably have her do. "I'm not going anywhere without you."

"At this rate," Lucia replied, "*neither* of us are going anywhere. I don't have long... And he can't always be watching me. He'll need to tell people something eventually. And when he does, I'll never be able to get out of here."

Agnete could feel her pulse quickening. *This is bad.* "There must be something we can do..." she wracked her brain for a solution. "We need to keep Bartrand from acting on his fears... Perhaps we can *assuage* his fears? Convince him that the situation isn't what he thinks it is? You're great at doing that- surely we can-"

"Agnete."

The flat way that she said her name sent a shiver down Agnete's skin.

"...I have to kill him."

She stared at Lucia. She had heard the words that left her mouth. But it was as though she couldn't understand them. "...No."

"What do you mean, *'no'*?"

"No," she repeated. "You can't."

"What other choice do I have?!" she pulled her arms away from Agnete's grasp. "I'll see him dead, take his money... Maybe we can escape-"

"Lucia- *please. No.*"

"How long, Agnete? How long until I become the woman in the attic?!" She rand a hand through her wind-tangled hair and anxiously scanned the spaces between the trees. When she turned back to Agnete, she could see the desperation shifting into a stone cold determination. She strode back over to Agnete, taking her face in her hand. "I will kill him with my bare hands," she said, "before I see him hurt a single hair on your head."

"You don't *need* to kill him." Agnete placed her own hand over Lucia's. "This is too much. The village will find out- there's no way that you can get away with this!"

"Not unless I use the right poison."

Time seemed to slow around them.

"No," Agnete said. "I won't help you. I won't take part in killing someone."

Lucia stood there silently. Agnete had expected her to try and change her mind. When she didn't, her legs felt like they might collapse underneath her.

The herbs.

No. Please, no. "You didn't."

"I've been putting aside some of the herbs," she admitted. "A little bit, every week. I have been since the beginning... Just in case. *Just as a last resort.*"

Agnete could feel the acid threatening to creep into the back of her throat. "You... *lied* to me?"

"I never *intended* on killing him!" Lucia followed Agnete as she backed away. "I only did it to have in case of an *emergency*. I *promise* you. And this is an emergency! I could be trapped here forever. And this could be *life or death* for you!" She caught Agnete's arm. "I'm sorry that I kept this from you. I'm sorry that I betrayed your trust in me. But I will *not* risk you getting hurt or worse."

Agnete shook her head. "There *has* to be another way-"

"Oh, come *on!* Agnete! He is a *terrible* man! He has confined me, decided to control who I can and can't see, where I can and can't go... *Yes*," she added when Agnete tried to speak, "It's because he's afraid. But that is *no* excuse."

"But death?" Agnete asked. "Some consequences for his actions, yes. But does he really deserve to *die?*"

Lucia shook her head, apologetic. "The risk is just too high." She took Agnete's hands in her own. "I *love* your heart. I love your softness and your compassion. But *I* am the one who has to endure his fear, day after day. I do *not* share your sympathy." Agnete watched the regret bloom in her eyes. "There is no other way."

She would have thought that the worst part of this conversation would have been the legitimacy with which they were discussing murder. Or perhaps the fact that the person she had grown to love most in the world had broken her trust and hidden it from her. But neither of these were the worst part.

No, she thought, *the single worst part of this whole conversation is the mirror it's holding up to my face.*

For all her moral and ethical objections, this had confirmed what Agnete had only suspected to be true for a long time: That she could deny Lucia nothing.

She covered her face with her hands. Lucia wasn't entirely wrong. But she wasn't prepared to live the rest of her life as a murderer. She wasn't prepared to let Lucia subject herself to that fate, either, no matter what she said.

"...What if I told you that there *was* another way?" Agnete asked through her fingers, almost too quiet to be heard.

Her mother hadn't shared every herb or concoction she of knew with her- some, she had to learn from the books she kept tucked away, where she thought Agnete wouldn't find them. She had asked her mother about lethean hemlock after she found a page on the plant in one of these books. Her mother had gone quiet, and spoke barely above a whisper for over a week. When she finally decided to answer Agnete's questions, she kept both hands on a warm mug of tea to keep them from shaking.

She had only ever used it once, she said. On a young child. She wouldn't say why. Only that she had truly thought that it was the right thing to do, considering the circumstances.

The child took the medicine in a cup of tea. They spent a few days recovering at her mother's home, the child's mother there with them the entire time. When they recovered, the child left and went on with their life. And Agnete's mother had regretted it ever since.

'It isn't worth it,' her mother had told her. *'It isn't worth the* what if's, *the time spent wondering what their life would have been like if they hadn't taken the hemlock. It isn't worth the lifetime of wondering whether you made the right decision. The mind is such a fragile thing...'* She looked to be somewhere far away, and when she returned, Agnete saw the heavy mist in her eyes. *'Don't ever use it, Agnete. Don't ever make the same mistake I did, sweet girl.'*

Agnete hesitated at least a dozen times as she told Lucia of her idea. She couldn't stop herself from wondering if she really was about to spend the rest of her life wondering if she did the right thing.

If I don't do this instead, Lucia might kill him.

If we leave Bartrand to his own devices, then- at best- we never see each other again. At worst, Lucia lives and dies here... And I...

They wouldn't really hurt me... Would they?

A predatory drum in her chest. *And yet. And yet. And yet.*

She hesitated. She explained her idea, her *plan*, to Lucia. She hesitated some more. Lucia just listened, eyes penetrating Agnete's composure.

"...Yes." Lucia said eventually. "Yes. Okay."

Agnete tried to keep her breath from shuddering. "...Are you sure?"

"Are you?"

No. No, I'm not.

Lucia pulled Agnete's cloak tight around her. "He's not a happy man, Agnete. Perhaps... this will be a kindness to him."

23

Agnete wanted to sit and wait calmly for Lucia and Bartrand's arrival. But she wasn't that kind of person. So she spent hours peering out her windows and putting her nervous energy into cleaning and checking on the doctored tea. The storm wasn't helping; it had started early in the evening, clouds choking the sky and warning gusts of wind reeling through the trees. Now it fell upon the woods in full force. Rain pummelled the ground, turning the dirt path into a muddy paste. Wind rapped on her windows like an impatient visitor. Thunder rumbled soft and low in the distance.

She jumped when the banging began on her door. Expecting it hadn't settled her nerves in the slightest.

When she opened the door, Bartrand stood glowering at her with Lucia in tow, her arm firmly held in his grasp. They were both soaking wet.

"I'm so sorry," she gasped at Agnete through a curtain of wet hair. "I tried to tell him-"

Agnete couldn't act like Lucia could. But the anger helped. "What is the meaning of this?" *He dragged her all the way here... in a thunderstorm.* Bartrand pushed past her, dragging Lucia in with him. She was shaking. Agnete grit her teeth- she didn't know if it was real, or if Lucia was just shivering for effect. Both thoughts made her feel viciously protective. Her blood grew hot under her skin. "Bold of you to enter a witch's home without an invitation."

"It was very bold of *you* to control my wife with your magic herbs!"

His speech was still faintly slurred, and he walked with a small slump to his spine. *He still hasn't fully recovered from the drinks Lucia drugged.*

Agnete took a deep breath and tried to affect a neutral tone. "Lucia and I are friends-"

"Oh, *spare me* the lies! I haven't the patience for any more of your games." He let go of Lucia, who backed into a nearby wall. Their clothes dripped around the wet footprints they left all over the floor as they moved. "You've spent months now making every effort to pull apart my life, thread by thread!"

"*Your* life?"

"Who else?!" he boomed. "You have made it your mission to discredit me. You've charmed my wife in an effort to influence me- don't look so surprised," he added when he saw her face. And it was true- she was surprised. But not for the reason he thought. "I know how politics work- You aren't as clever as you think you are. Who else, if not me? *Lucia?*" he scoffed. "That you could be so jealous of her that you'd seduce her into being your friend?" Agnete stiffened, trying not to blush at his choice of words. "Perhaps. Perhaps that was *part* of it. But I don't think that your motivations were so childish. So tell me now. Why? What is it that drove you to try and ruin my life? What is it that you want?!"

Lucia beheld her from behind her husband. "You don't have to tell him anything-"

"*Silence!*"

"My reasons are my own," Agnete replied, forcing her back to straighten against its will.

"You think you have the upper hand tonight? You think you have *any* leverage?" Bartrand stalked over to her. "Believe you me, you have *nothing*. I could rally the entire village to your doorstep in a matter of hours. So tell me what it is that you want!"

Agnete clenched her teeth and remained silent.

"Answer me!"

The best lies have a little bit of truth to them, Lucia had told her.

And yet. And yet. And yet.

They want me to be the villain? They want me to be the monster?

Fine.

"You want the truth?" Her voice dropped, fell into somewhere dark.

"My entire life, I've been relegated to the outside. I saw how my mother was treated. I saw how she was ignored, avoided, scorned until someone needed something from her.

"I was with her when she died. *Alone.* Did you know that not a single person came to pay their respects? Or to bring her food? Or to give her the comfort of conversation? Not a *single* one. This village has been cruel to us- *worse* than cruel. My mother died cold and alone, abandoned by the very people she dedicated decades of her life to healing. To *comforting.* And this was the thanks she received- not a soul in the world to spare a thought for her. Not a soul except for her one and only daughter, born only to share the same *miserable* fate as her.

"I decided that I couldn't do it. I wouldn't. If I couldn't have love, or gratitude, or simple kindness, then I would settle for fear. And power." The falsehood sat like lead in her gut, growing with every lie she added and making her stomach churn. "Yes. I gave Lucia those fertility herbs. I told her that if all went well, she would conceive before long. Very likely, she would bear twins. And that in exchange, one of those children would be given to me."

Bartrand laughed, a bitter sound, in time with the rain hitting Agnete's roof. "You think you would have gotten away with stealing a baby? From under my own roof?"

"We had a good plan- didn't we, Lucia?" Her friend looked appropriately reminiscent of a startled deer. "It's surprisingly simple, taking a baby. Witches have been doing it for centuries." That particular sentence tasted sour in her mouth. "There are many ways to quiet a newborn for a short time. And you're a busy man... easily kept away from the birth of your children by urgent village business. If Lucia could not bring me the child herself, then it would have been an easy matter to bewitch one of her midwives." In a stroke of sagacity, she gestured in the direction of the barn outside. "I even had a barn built," she added, "For goats' milk.

"I would quietly raise the child here. And when the time was right, I would either blackmail or extort you. If I can't acquire the respect of the village myself... then I figured that you could do it for me."

Bartrand stood mute, regarding her with less contempt than Agnete was expecting. He turned and looked at Lucia, who peered up at him through her eyelashes, practised tears waiting in the corners of her eyes like ammunition. He sighed, a rough gale of a sound, and turned his attention back to Agnete.

"...I'm not heartless, you know," he said. "I'm not a fool. I'm not the unreasonable man you might believe me to be.

"I understand. To be rejected and cast out by your peers... I can merely imagine the isolation. The pain." He inclined his head and looked her in the eyes, jaw set. "I see before me a wretched thing. And I pity you.

"But you chose this path," he said. "You could have changed how they see you. *Well-* I suppose you did try. But you could have done it the *right* way. You could have been honest. You could have made yourself more friendly, more approachable. You could have made an effort to be a *part* of the village, rather than hide yourself away in the woods day after day. You could have *cared* about the people around you, instead of caring only for what they can do for you." He shook his head. "You could have been good. But you chose this path, instead." He began to turn on his heel. "I ought to inform my constituents..."

Lucia tried to grab his arm. "Husband, no- *please-*"

Agnete saw the threat for what it was. But it wasn't what had her frozen in place, shaking with rage. *"Don't,"* she protested, fighting with the every last fraying fibre of her being to restrain herself.

Despite her proximity, Lucia's voice sounded distant and fuzzy in Agnete's head. "Darling- *please.* If I love you for anything, for any of your many qualities, it is your *heart.* Please, I beg you- have mercy-"

Desperation, executed to perfection. A clap of thunder reverberated in the woods. Her pleas finally cracked Bartrand's resolve. He ripped his arm from his wife and spun back around.

"Break your hold on my wife!" he demanded, voice just starting to break. "It pains me to hear her beg on behalf of someone who has only used her!"

The last scrap of control Agnete had over herself disappeared. A lifetime of hurt and loneliness began to corrode her insides, burning away every organ in her body until there was nothing left but wrath.

"Maybe I shouldn't."

Bartrand's mouth curled back, his teeth glaring at her. She didn't care.

"Why should I bother, if you're just going to sic the village on me?" she asked him, her voice plunging the room into cold. She was only dimly aware of the look of confusion on Lucia's face. "If my fate is sealed, then what do I have to lose?"

He couldn't conceal the disquieted darting of his eyes. "You're bluffing."

"Are you willing to find out?

"Go ahead. Have me strung up. Drowned. Burned. Chase me away, if you're feeling merciful. I won't even need to curse you. You'll have deprived the village of its only healer. The blood of every preventable death will be on your hands. It won't be long before your people turn on you, next. And the woman you love will spend her life hating you, grieving my loss until death sees fit to relieve her of her heartbreak."

Lucia was trying to get her attention now, giving her the most urgent look she could manage. *What the fuck are you doing?* It demanded.

"But maybe I'll curse you, anyways," Agnete continued. "Just because I can." Lucia was shaking her head now, droplets of water falling from the ends of her hair, an inaudible *no* repeating on her lips. "Tell me, Bartrand... Do you want to know what it feels like, to breathe your last breath without a single person in the world to care?"

He retreated backwards, beholding her as he would a demon come to life. "...What do you want?" The question came out in a whisper.

"You know what I want. What is it that *you* want?" a malevolent smile teased her lips. "I'm not the unreasonable woman you might believe me to be."

When he didn't speak or move, she moved deliberately over to the chairs in front of the hearth. She glared at him. "Please. Sit." *It's bad luck to deny a witch's hospitality. I can threaten you, too.* When he submitted, she repeated the question and sat across from him. Lucia had grown quiet, watching them cautiously from the wall. "What do you want?"

There was a tremble to his words. "Break your hold on my wife. Leave this place and never come back."

"The first is not an issue. But the second... Believe what you will about me. But I will not abandon these people to illness and injury. What do you *really* want?"

"For you to be gone-"

"Why do you want me gone?"

He sputtered. "Y-You can't be serious-"

"Why do you want me gone?"

"You are *ruining* my life-!"

"How am I ruining your life?"

He began to shout. "You've bewitched my *fucking wife-*"

"How is that ruining your life?"

"You have made me a fool!"

"Why should it matter if you're a fool?"

"Are you-"

"Why should it matter if you're a fool?"

"Because no one respects a fucking fool!" he erupted, shooting to his feet and flipping the chair behind him. "No one *trust* a fool- not to do what needs to be done, and not to know what he's talking about! Nobody takes a *fool* seriously! I will not be duped! I will not be *humiliated!* I will not be made to feel incapable-" his voice cracked- "Stupid..."

Agnete sat motionless in her chair. "You don't want to be inferior."

"...I will not have them believe me an *unworthy man.*"

"But *you* believe it." Agnete watched him, standing heaving and wordless. "What do you want, Bartrand?"

He shuddered and pressed the heels of his palms to his eyes. Wind gently rattled the windows around them. On the other side of the glass, branches trembled against the panes, *tap-tap-tapping* like fingernails. *"... I just want to be happy. I have never been happy.*

"I-It's just a target that keeps moving, isn't it?" He asked. "Just when you think you're close enough to touch it, it isn't there anymore. It's gone, like a mirage. Or a dream you can't remember when you wake in the morning. And somehow, everyone else seems to reach it. Not just once, but *over and over again...* And I don't know how they do it. I don't know why it doesn't disappear for them like it does for me." The breath seemed to leave his lungs as he leaned on the wall by the hearth. He looked as though he would deflate and sink to the floor at any moment. "...I'm old. Too old to keep reaching for a moving target," he said. "I don't care how I find it. I don't care *why* I find it. I don't care if it's with a spell or a potion or a bloody sacrifice. I'm tired of existing the hard way. I just want the simple way."

Agnete's voice eased into something resembling sympathy. "I understand."

She slowly rose from her chair and crossed the floor to the teapot keeping warm by the fire. She picked it up, brought it to a trio of mugs- one with a sleeve- and poured the contents into a single cup. She brought the drink over to Bartrand. "Would you like a drink?"

He accepted the mug mechanically, not remembering until he raised it to his lips to exercise caution. He looked down into the cloudy, earth-green liquid and hesitated.

"It won't kill you, if that's what you're thinking."

The mug remained suspended in his hand, his eyes searching its contents for guidance.

Agnete stepped back over to the table and made to fill the other two cups. She took a steadying breath, choosing her words carefully. "It won't hurt," she said. "It's just a drink."

Moments later, Bartrand lost consciousness and collapsed to the floor. She and Lucia both ran to his crumpled body, stepping over small puddles and sharp pieces of broken ceramic. Lucia heaved his head onto her lap when the shaking started. Agnete hadn't lied- the convulsions wouldn't be painful for him. But she found herself wishing that they were.

She thought that this should scare her. She thought that her desire to see someone in pain should, logically and morally speaking, terrify her.

"Should" was a distant thing.

She gripped his ankles and held them in place as hard as she could against the floor. Her fingers squeezed into his legs, nails digging into his flesh through his clothes. She wasn't aware of the tears streaking down her face as they waited for the worst to be over. A feral sound started to bubble up inside her. She squeezed her eyes shut- a growl turned into a roar as Bartrand shook beneath her, her hands pinning him down with everything she had.

She was still crying and burning when he stilled moments later. She hadn't noticed- she was the one shaking, now. Her vision was too blurred and too scarlet for her to see Lucia lifting Bartrand's head from her lap and crawling over to her. Agnete only dimly recognized her presence when she felt palms on her damp, searing hot cheeks.

"Hey," she said. *"Hey. Listen to me."* She sounded far away. *"I'm here. I'm here."*

Agnete just started to cry harder.

"It's okay. I'm here. Just breathe. Just breathe with me. Just slow down."

The world had disappeared. She only realized the feeling of *void* around her when the world started to come back and refill the darkness.

"That's it. Keep breathing. In, and out. In, and out. Try it just a little bit slower. I'm right here. I'm not going anywhere."

With every exhale, Lucia's voice became closer. Her touch solidified into more than just a faint buzzing on her skin.

"Good... just a little bit slower. In... and out."

When she was able to open her eyes, Lucia wiped the tears from Agnete's cheeks with her thumbs. She cradled Agnete in her arms and murmured reassurances into her hair while she cried.

24

They made up a pallet bed for Bartrand in the barn. There wasn't enough room for him in the cottage. They kept the barn doors locked at night, barred from the outside, just in case he woke up while they were asleep. Agnete always left a lantern burning inside for him, just in case.

Lucia went into town during the days, making enough of an appearance to keep suspicion at bay. She dishevelled herself a tiny bit more each day, to better play the part of a woman exhausted from worrying and caring for her bedridden husband.

"No one's said anything?" Agnete asked for the hundredth time when Lucia arrived back at the barn. "No one suspects anything?"

"No, I don't think so." Lucia dropped her cloak onto the back of a chair Agnete had moved into the barn. She fell backwards into the seat, sighing.

"I'm sorry you have to spend the days in that house, all by yourself."

"It's not so bad. At least I'm sleeping better, now."

"Are you sure-" Agnete hesitated, reconsidering the question she wanted to ask. "...You're not avoiding me?"

"Why would I be avoiding you?"

"When Bartrand-" she licked her lips. "When I..."

"When we poisoned him."

She flinched. "I... wasn't myself."

Lucia leaned forward in the chair. "What makes you say that?" she asked. When Agnete didn't answer, she said, "Just because you don't like a part of yourself, doesn't mean it isn't still a part of you. You can't disown parts of your heart." She reached out and took Agnete's hands in her own. "I'm not afraid of you. Not even when you're like that."

But I *am.* "The way you looked at me..."

"I was... *surprised*," she said, pulling back and straightening herself.

"Good surprised, or bad surprised?"

Lucia pursed her lips in thought. Agnete could see the calculations playing out behind her eyes. A slow fear began creeping up her back, her neck, and into her skull as she waited for Lucia to answer the question.

Just as Lucia opened her mouth, a disoriented grumble came from the pallet bed.

They shared a look before darting towards Bartrand.

Lethean hemlock was ultimately a neurotoxin. While the effects on the peripheral nervous system were mild, those who ingested a sufficiently distilled amount suffered from long- and short-term memory loss. Sometimes complete, sometimes not. But almost always permanent.

"What will he remember?" Lucia asked.

"It's unpredictable... Perhaps a lot. Perhaps a little. Perhaps nothing."

Lucia sat on the edge of the pallet bed as Bartrand gradually came to. When he was conscious enough to speak, his words came out in groggy fragments.

"...Where am I?"

"Do you remember your name?" Lucia asked. *Wasting no time,* Agnete thought. *As though I'd expect any less.*

He knit his brows, perplexed at the simple question. Painstakingly, his lips began to form a shape. His voice began to give life to the shape. "B... B..." he made the sound to himself, experimenting with the feel of it in his mouth. "...Bart...*Bart*," he decided.

'Bart'... A nickname? A childhood name?

Lucia kept her face impassive. "What is that short for?"

He squinted, concentrating on a knot in the floor as though it might have the answer. When he couldn't find it, he became distracted, surveying the room. "...Where am I?"

Lucia reached out to console him. "You're safe. You're-"

"What happened?" He grew agitated, raising his voice and backing into his pillow. "Why am I here?! What am I doing here, what happened-" He halted when he caught sight of Lucia's face. "Oh... I'm... so sorry... I've scared you... My..." he pondered her. Agnete eyes widened and met Lucia's in a brief, shared glance. "My..."

"Your daughter," Lucia improvised, taking one of his hands. "I'm your daughter, papa. You remember- thank the Goddess, you remember-" she pressed her forehead to his fingers. "She said you might not remember... She said you might not wake up. Thank the Goddess-"

"*She*..." he found Agnete standing a safe distance away. A look of confusion, then fear passed over his features. His breath grew fast and heavy. He started clambering back on the bed, limbs still clumsy from days of sleep. Agnete was pinned to the spot, panicking.

"Calm yourself!" Lucia exclaimed. "It's alright-"

"I don't... I don't want to-"

"Of course not, of course not-" she made an emphatic attempt to stroke his arms. "It makes perfect sense- of course you feel that way! She looks so much like her mother-" she looked pointedly at Agnete- "Your sister?" she asked him. "Do you remember your sister, papa?"

His limbs grew heavy again. He shook his head.

Lucia feigned resignation. "Perhaps that's for the best..." she said. "You were... *estranged.*"

Bart rolled the word around in his mouth. "*Sister...*"

"You never spoke about her... not even when I asked you. You wouldn't speak of her, or why the two of you never spoke."

He gulped. "Is she... here?"

She shook her head. "No... she died some time ago. This-" she gestured to Agnete- "is her daughter. Your niece. She looks so much like her. But she won't hurt you."

Did she have this thought out, already? Agnete wondered, *Or is she making this all up on the spot?* She wouldn't have put either past Lucia's capabilities.

"...What happened to me?" he repeated. "Why can't I remember?"

Agnete felt responsible for answering at least one of his questions. "You fell off of your horse. You were going too fast through the woods. You fell into the ravine, just to the North-East. We brought you back here. We didn't know if you would wake up."

"And we're so glad that you have," Lucia added. "We'll take you to see a doctor in the city when you're well enough for the trip."

There it was: Bart's final destination. When he was well enough, Lucia would acquire a cart. She would take enough of Bart's money to see them through until he could be placed somewhere he'd be taken care of. Then they would make the journey back to the village, where- presumably- Lucia would pass herself off as the Mayor's widow.

It wasn't a perfect plan. Agnete lost sleep poring over it. But Bart would be alive, with a chance at happiness somewhere new. And Lucia would have his home, his library, and the rest of his money all to herself. It wasn't the escape that she dreamt of... But it was more freedom than she'd ever had.

25

It took longer than expected for Bart to recover. Agnete attributed it to his age- his body couldn't be expected to heal as quickly as a child's.

They had expected Bart to be a relatively different person, without a lifetime of memories to shape his identity. But the change was still startling. It chilled Agnete to think that, in a way, they *had* killed him... just like Lucia had originally planned. Bartrand was dead. Bart now inhabited the body he left behind.

Lucia continued to spend her days being seen in the village. This left Agnete to care for Bart by herself until nightfall. Lucia offered to help shoulder his care, but the timing made it difficult for them to share the responsibility.

The guilt bore down on Agnete while she cared for Bart. He asked for his daughter often, and she had to tell him that Lucia was in town, taking care of his business. They were both careful not to reveal too much about their location, choosing their words carefully and being as vague as reasonably possible. When he asked what his business was, Agnete panicked and said that she wasn't sure; *"I never understood it,"* she told him. She ended up looking rather silly when Lucia told him that it was barkeeping.

"You just wanted to have a joke at my expense, didn't you?" Agnete asked her when they had returned to the cottage that evening.

"No," Lucia answered, a small smirk betraying her. She admitted, sheepishly, "I wanted to pick something I thought he might actually like, in his twilight years." Her eyes flicked to Agnete, then away again. "You're rubbing off on me, sweetling."

-

When the time came to leave for the city, Lucia left the cottage well before the sun rose in the morning. She arrived later with a cart and a pair of horses.

"They took pity on me and lent them to me," she told Agnete, not bothering to say who "they" were.

They had little more than a set of general directions to get to the city; the journey took so long that it was rare for anyone to travel there, and rarer still for anyone *from* the city to venture out to the village. They departed as the sun rose, luggage and provisions piled in the cart with them. It gave Agnete anxiety leaving behind her home, despite knowing that it was temporary. She tried and failed to keep from looking back over her shoulder. When she hazarded a glance at Lucia, she found her eyes fixed straight ahead, expression stony as she held the reigns on the horses.

The road leading away from the village was a rough, neglected path marked by splodges of grass and moss. Thick, woody roots occasionally peered out from the dirt, making the first days of their journey slow and uncomfortable. Eventually, they reached another road: a thicker dirt road, with more bumps and puddles than were comfortable, but a more travel-worn one than the first. They would see other travellers on this road, though they were very few and very far-between. They continued to ride as far as the horses would take them, stopping every night to make camp. Lucia expressed several times how useless she felt when it came time to make a fire and set up their bedrolls. Agnete pretended not to notice her sulkiness when she failed at the simplest tasks. Even Bart was capable of setting up a simple tent on his own. He offered to teach Lucia how to tie the proper knots and set the stakes into the ground.

"He believes he's my father. He's probably just pleased to teach me something. I'm just humouring him."

Agnete didn't quite believe her. She felt a strange sort of relief, however, watching them interact; with Bart's memory of her gone, she wasn't putting nearly as much effort into upholding the syrup-sweet mask she had always worn around him.

"How does it feel, being away from home?" Lucia asked her one night as they lay in their bedrolls, fire crackling outside their tent.

"Nerve-wracking," Agnete replied truthfully. She shifted onto her side, facing Lucia. "How does it feel, being away from home?"

A sardonic snort escaped her. "Freeing," she sighed. "It's not home. Not really. I was just born there."

"So you haven't found your home, yet."

Lucia rolled her head to the side, towards Agnete. Agnete waited for her to reply as Lucia studied her for a long moment. Finally, Lucia turned her head back towards the top of the tent. "Maybe."

Agnete didn't know what *'maybe'* meant.

Outside, Bart was regarding a small rabbit with curiosity. He watched it, seemingly charmed with the creature, and extended a hand towards it when it hopped slightly nearer. Startled, the rabbit sprinted away. Bart looked after it, a look of sadness on his face.

Eventually, they reached another road. This one was smoothed with cobblestones worn into the hard-packed earth, and ran parallel to the West ridge of the mountains. Here, they found more comfortable places to break and sleep, near rivers and in small clearings carved into the trees. The city was near the coast, allowing them to enjoy more errant breezes and the calls of seabirds as they neared their destination. It almost made up for the increased frequency of other travellers on the road. Agnete couldn't help feeling disappointed- she had grown so used to the solitude with Lucia *(and, admittedly, Bart)* that the roads had begun to feel like their own private world to traverse together.

Lucia was practically buzzing when the city appeared on the horizon. It lingered in their line of sight for hours. Agnete noticed Lucia getting more and more fidgety as they approached, rubbing the reins between her fingers and bouncing her heel beneath her. She was quiet, speaking very little as she watched the buildings grow ever closer.

There were no gates looming over them, nor walls to mark their transition into the foreign place. They weren't in the city... then suddenly they were. It seemed to swallow them up, lamppost -lined streets twisting them deeper between brick and whitewash buildings. The crowds of people had their own current, making it harder and harder to navigate the streets in their cart.

Eventually, they found somewhere to unload. Agnete watched as Lucia asked a man for directions, unable to hear their exchange over the noise of the street.

"People here are quite rude," Lucia remarked when she got back.

"Oh, no."

Lucia shrugged. "Better than being politely disingenuous."

Following the directions they were given, they managed to find an inn nearby. They paid for two rooms: One for Bart, and another for themselves.

"Are you sure he'll be okay on his own?" Agnete asked after the got him settled.

133

"He'll be fine. If he didn't try to make off on the way here, then he won't try it now." Lucia dropped a heavy bag into the corner of their small room. "Besides... he wouldn't abandon his daughter. And his niece."

"If you say so."

"I do. And on that note-" She planted her hands on her hips. "Let's bring the old man some dinner, then go back out."

"Why would you want to go back out? Aren't you tired?"

"I want to eat street food," she resolved. "I saw a stall on the way here. I want to try it."

Not half an hour later, Agnete was watching Lucia shove tendrils of pasta into her mouth. She couldn't stop herself from smiling at how the sauce splattered around her lips- she had never seen Lucia eat less delicately than she did now. Lucia hummed contentedly as every other mouthful went down her throat. Agnete almost didn't taste her own dinner- Lucia's pleasure in the novelty of her dinner was too distracting.

Later, they changed into nightdresses and crawled under the covers of their shared bed for the night, lying next to each other. It wasn't as comfortable as Agnete's bed at home, but after so many nights sleeping in a bedroll on the ground, it felt luxurious.

Lucia fixed her attention on her. "Bartrand's gone-"

"*Bart.*"

She sighed. "*Bart* is gone. We can speak freely."

"Alright."

"You've been... distant," Lucia said. "Well- not distant, exactly. But... preoccupied. What's wrong?"

'Wrong'. All things considered- in a *bigger-picture* sort of way- Agnete didn't think that there was a lot that was *'wrong'.*

She had saved Bart's life. He'd now have the chance to find something resembling happiness here in the city, rather than meeting the early grave that Lucia had resolved for him. It had cost him dearly... but Agnete hoped that it would be worth it.

Lucia was experiencing a taste of the liberation she craved.

Despite the circumstances- questionable, at best- she felt as though she was sharing a new adventure with her best friend. There was a freedom in this place, where they didn't need to sneak around or hide their affection for one another. No one leered at her as she went about her business, or stared as she and Lucia walked arm in arm.

Lucia was right, however. She had been preoccupied. She hadn't had the capacity to sort out her thoughts or let her feelings breathe before now- she had been constantly on edge, scared of being found out. The comfortable quiet of long days spent on the road gave her space to reflect.

She was coming to realize that she felt loved in a way that she hadn't, before.

She was coming to realize just how *seen* she felt- the kind of deep, reciprocal seeing that made you feel as though the two of you held an entire, secret world between you.

She was coming to realize that the face across from her was the one that she wanted to wake up to morning after morning after morning.

She was coming to realize what it meant when every part of you ached when someone wasn't nearby.

Her mother had told her that love was a complicated thing. But she was wrong.

Agnete was coming to realize that being in love wasn't complicated... it was the simplest thing in the world. It was the rest of life that was complicated.

"Is this about the night when Bart drank the tea?"

Agnete blinked back into the present. *No. Well... maybe a little bit.* "...Yes."

"Still?" Lucia asked. "I told you... I'm not scared of your tears. Or your screams. Or your anger."

"But I am."

"Why?"

"I don't like feeling that way," she answered. "I don't like losing control of myself. I'm scared of what I might do, when I'm like that... I'm scared that I might hurt someone. It makes me feel like a rabid dog that needs to be put down."

Lucia stroked her arm. "I think it feels that way because you never *let* yourself get angry. I think you take all of that anger and push it down so far that it has no way to get out. It just stays there and keeps getting bigger. And when it does come up, all of it comes out at once.

"You need to feel your anger, when it happens. You need to let it escape, somehow."

"But what if it turns me into a monster?" Agnete asked. "What if I lose control of myself?"

"You won't," she reassured her. "But if you do, I'll be here to bring you back to yourself again."

That was it. What was truly wrong.

That one day, she wouldn't be there to bring her back. Or to laugh with her. Or to be the first person to share her excitement with. Or to look over her shoulder at a cute animal Agnete pointed out to her. Or to tell her that she was going overboard and making too much food for two people. Or to need her in some way.

What was wrong was that one day, she wouldn't be there at all.

"...Can I tell you something?" Lucia asked. Agnete nodded. "You promise not to let it go to your head?" she nodded again, smiling. "...I'm glad you convinced me not to kill Bart."

Warmth bloomed in Agnete's chest. "Thank you for telling me that."

"I mean it."

She laced her fingers into Lucia's. "I'll always be here to bring you back to yourself, too." She paused before a small laugh drifted through her nose. "Even when you're a mean little fox."

"Nooo!" Lucia leaned back and wauled.

"It's too late."

"You would deny me my *one joy* in the afterlife-"

"There's no backing out, now. You already promised. You've sworn yourself in."

"This is why no one trusts you witches."

"Wow."

Lucia covered her mouth as her small snort bubbled into a laugh. Agnete stretched her little finger towards her.

"Foxes."

"Foxes."

-

Lucia was still sleeping when Agnete awoke from the best night's sleep she'd had in weeks. The small window in their room cast a thin beam of light over the length of Lucia's hair and onto her arm. The heat they shared under the blanket was impossibly comfortable. It

137

was unbearably difficult for Agnete to pull back the cover and tear herself away.

After she dressed, she tiptoed over to the door and snuck out of the room, quietly closing the door behind her. She padded to the neighbouring room to check in on Bart.

When she tested the door, she was surprised to find it unlocked. She opened it a crack at first, in case Bart was still asleep. When she didn't see his form on the mattress, she opened the door wider and cautiously called his name.

She stepped inside and scanned the room. He was nowhere to be seen. Her pulse quickened. Fear sparked in her chest.

She bolted back into her and Lucia's room.

"Lucia- wake up-"

Lucia made a noise of protest at Agnete's gentle jostling. She rubbed her eyes and grumbled an inarticulate question at Agnete.

"Bart's gone-"

"What?"

"He's gone, I don't know where he is-" Agnete's words started running into each other.

"He's not in his room?"

"*No, he's gone!*"

"Shh- alright-" She inhaled sharply- "Is it possible that his memory came back?"

"I- Maybe? I don't think so, but..."

"Let me get dressed... We'll find him."

Once she had enough clothes on, Agnete pulled Lucia out of their room. Lucia made directly for the stairs.

"Should we check his room for clues?" Agnete asked.

"I don't think we'll find any." Agnete followed her down the stairs, taking them two at a time. "Just- come on. Let's go, we'll take a walk around-"

Lucia stopped suddenly at the foot of the stairs, making Agnete run into her. Agnete stumbled, peering around Lucia to see what had frozen her in her tracks.

Bart was sitting at one of the long wooden tables, spreading honey onto a thick slice of bread, a half-empty bowl of porridge in front of him.

Lucia pressed two fingers to the space between her eyebrows. "You didn't think to check downstairs?"

"I'm sorry..." Agnete tried to keep the waver from her voice. "I panicked..."

Lucia sighed softly before turning her body towards her. "Come here," she said, opening her arms and wrapping them around Agnete.

From Lucia's shoulder, Agnete heard footsteps approaching them. "That's your father?" a man's voice asked. Agnete pulled away and saw the innkeeper looking at them.

"Yes," Lucia answered.

"He said that you and your wife would be paying for his food when you came down. Is that right?"

Agnete's face heated. "We're not-"

Lucia did a better job of concealing the colour in her cheeks than Agnete did. "Yes. That's right," she replied stiffly. "I have the coinpurse. I'll pay."

After she compensated the innkeeper, she drew the drawstrings tight and replaced it on her hip. "We'll take him to see a doctor after breakfast," she said, avoiding Agnete's eyes. "We'll get him placed somewhere he'll be taken care of... Maybe find him something to occupy his time."

Agnete nodded at the ground, begging the colour to fade from her cheeks.

26

The doctors didn't question the story about Bart falling off of his horse. They had no reason to. For all of their knowledge on surgery, diseases, and the latest medical interventions, they weren't well-versed in herbalism or spellwork. That's why people like Agnete were still able to make a living.

When Agnete finished seeing Bart situated in his room and speaking with one of the doctors, she found Lucia sitting on a bench with an old woman. The medical facility was built with a small courtyard in the centre, lined with a loggia on each side to protect patients, visitors, and attendees from the rain. When Lucia saw her, she bid farewell to the woman on the bench and made her way to Agnete.

"Who was that?"

"No one in particular. She was here visiting her husband. She was just saying hello."

There was something off about Lucia after they left the building. Agnete thought that she might be worried about Bart regaining his memory or about the doctors discovering what they had done. But when she asked, Lucia had denied feeling concerned about either.

If it were Agnete acting unusual, Lucia would have asked her outright what was bothering her. But that wasn't Agnete's way. So she waited as they went about their day, hoping that Lucia would open up to her in her own time.

"What would you like to have for dinner?" Agnete asked. They had been strolling the streets together again, leisurely exploring the streets and hidden crevices of the city. Now they meandered through the worn stone paths of a cemetery just off a busy road. The large trees lining the paths quieted the sounds of the street, and weepy branches softened the high sun overhead. Rows and clusters of tomb markers were dusted with a light coating of leaves. Flowers and small mementos for the dead peeked out from behind an eclectic mix of gravestones. Within the stone-and-iron gates, the world felt quiet. "Did you want to go to a food stall again?"

"I need to tell you something."

Just like that. No blunt-edged *'Agnete'*. No preamble. "Anything."

Lucia licked her lips. "They didn't give me the horses and the cart."

Agnete puzzled over the words. "They didn't give you..."

"The horses. Or the cart. I stole them while everyone was asleep."

Why would you have needed to? "Is it because they wouldn't have given it to you? Because of their distrust of me?"

"No. Nobody even knew that I was taking him to the city. No one knew that we were going anywhere. And that's not all. I didn't just take some of Bart's money, to see us here and back comfortably." She took a deep breath. "I took all of it."

It didn't take long for Agnete to put the pieces together. When she did, her heart sank. "...You were never planning on coming back."

"No," she admitted. Her breath hitched. "And... I'm such a bloody fool. I... I think I hoped that you would stay with me." A cord yanked and reverberated in Agnete's chest as Lucia's voice began to waver. "I know you couldn't... with the village, and your mother. But I let myself hope, anyways. Like a bloody *fucking* fool, and now I feel so stupid-"

141

Agnete deflated- watching Lucia slowly lose her composure hurt more than the lie. "You should have told me."

"But I didn't!" Her voice cracked and she rubbed an arm over her eyes. "That's who I am. I'm *selfish*. I was self-indulgent. I let myself hope, but was too scared to make a real plan. Because I knew that if I tried to make a plan, I would have seen that it wasn't possible! I can't even support you when the money runs out- and it's running out faster than I thought. *So much faster.* Everything costs so much *more* here. And the costs of getting Bart situated... I know," she added, "It's the right thing to do." The admission made Agnete feel an unexpected swell of pride in Lucia. "But the cost... it's too much. The money is going to run out. *Soon.*"

"I would never have expected you to support me."

"I know you wouldn't. But... *Goddess.* Do you have any idea what it feels like? To have spent your entire life being trained to be nothing more than a wife? To have ambition, but nowhere to put it? To be so useless that the mere notion of independence is unattainable?" The tears were too many now to keep off of her cheeks. "I tried *so hard-*"

Agnete pulled Lucia to her chest and held her there. The embrace only seemed to make her shake harder.

That's why you never left, she thought. *Isn't it?*

Because under all of that brilliance, you didn't think you were truly capable.

Because you didn't really believe you could do it.

"I've gotten us into such a mess... And you have always been *nothing* but good to me. You have always been honest with me. And I haven't been honest with you at all," Lucia cried.

"It's alright-"

"No, it's not," she insisted, pulling herself away from Agnete's shoulder. It made Agnete want to weep, seeing her eyes so red. A bird chirped from somewhere in the trees. Lucia sniffed. "I love you, Agnete."

For a fleeting second, Agnete let herself pretend. Too quickly, the euphoric fluttering was cut short by a stabbing pain through her heart.

Of course. You're my best friend. Back to reality. "I love you, too."

"You *aren't. Hearing me.*" Her hands gripped Agnete's arms, fingers digging into her flesh through the sleeves. "You are the most selfless, compassionate person I've ever met. You're everything I'm not. You're so giving and reflective, and you're not endlessly unsatisfied with the world. Sometimes I feel like I'm just this hunger, this *bottomless pit,* that just searches and dreams and takes, and is never sated. But you don't search and take- you just *give*, even to people who probably don't deserve it, purely because they need it. You just keep making the world a brighter place without questioning if you should. I feel so unworthy of being your friend, sometimes. And I've never felt unworthy of anything before in my life."

"You're not unworthy." She pushed Lucia's hair behind her ears, damp strands coming away from her cheeks. "*Never.*"

"I'm sorry... *I'm so sorry.* I don't want to ruin our friendship. I love our friendship. It means more to me than you'll ever know. *You* mean more to me than you'll ever know. But I *feel...*" Her eyes searched Agnete's, helpless. *"I love you."*

Agnete's heart was suddenly in her throat, choking her. *Why are you so hard to read? Why am I so oblivious? How have we wasted so much time hiding from each other?*

That wasn't true. It couldn't be. Time with Lucia had never felt wasted. Rather, time without her had grown to feel empty.

She put an arm around Lucia's waist to steady her. She fought the pins prickling at the corners of her eyes. "I love *you*."

Lucia's hand flew reflexively to her lips as a single, hysterically choked laugh popped from her mouth. Agnete took it in her own, folding her fingers into Lucia's palm. Lucia reached up and ran a thumb along Agnete's cheeks.

"Stop crying."

"*You* stop crying."

They laughed despite themselves. Agnete sniffled, drying her cheeks. She looked at Lucia, too light to notice her heart beating out of her chest. "...Can I kiss you?"

Lucia's fingers tightened on hers as she nodded. Agnete inclined her head and pulled Lucia towards her, inching closer until there was no more space between them.

27

It didn't feel like the end of their friendship. It felt like a full realization of what their friendship had always been.

They woke up the next morning still holding each other. They couldn't keep their hands apart while they ate breakfast, feeding themselves one-handed and smiling at each other from across the table. They took their time getting to the sanitarium afterwards, periodically pulling each other into convenient crevices between buildings just to kiss one another, as though they were trying to make up for lost opportunities. There was a high in being able to do so out in the open and going unremarked. There was a rush in knowing that hundreds of people could see them, and no one cared. There would be no gossiping, scowling, or staring. Just anonymous strangers walking past them, not knowing or caring who they were to each other.

When they arrived at the hospital, they learned that Bart had settled in comfortably and was already "making friends" among the older patients. He would be kept there until he was well enough to find other lodgings and some way to support himself. He didn't seem to mind that he wouldn't return to his "business" from before he lost his memory. His only complaint seemed to be that they didn't serve enough meat for supper.

On their way out from their visit, they noticed the old woman strolling through the loggia, carrying a bouquet of flowers wrapped in paper.

"Razivia," Lucia chirped, "What a lovely surprise!" She turned to Agnete. "You might remember, we were chatting the other day. Razivia visits every day to see her husband."

Agnete turned to the old woman. "I'm so sorry. He must be quite ill."

"That's alright," she replied with a weary, good-natured sigh. "That's what happens, when you get old. We've been married for nearly fifty years now, you know. Still madly in love. I picked a good one," she chuckled. "Comes with the territory, I suppose."

"And you brought him flowers," Lucia said. "That's so sweet."

"Oh- no, these are mine." Razivia jostled the blooms in her arm. "One of the doctors was a client of mine- him and his husband. They celebrate their anniversary, and I'm the one who gets the flowers..." She unfolded the paper with a sedate hand. "Here- take some."

Agnete lifted her hand in protest. "Oh, we couldn't possibly-"

"Please. I *insist*. I get these all the time. The house is absolutely bursting with them. You'd be doing me a favour."

Lucia smiled. "That's so kind of you."

"Just don't go giving them to your old man in there," she replied with a wink. "I don't need the doctor seeing them and thinking I've gone and given them away."

The blooms gave their small room at the inn a much-needed burst of colour. They sat near the window, poised to catch the light at every angle.

When the trees began to submerge the sun, they ventured towards the upper crest of the city. They walked until they found themselves on a road on a hill, lined on one side with a thick stone fence to keep pedestrians from falling onto the roofs of the buildings below. They stood between the dimly-glowing lampposts and leaned on the ledge of the fence, idly looking down at the city below them. A lazy, crisp wind blew past them, carrying suggestions of smoke and street food with it. By the time they started their games of *what-if,* the moon was out in its full splendour, spying on them like a knowing smile.

"What about that one?" Agnete asked, pointing at another distant house. They were standing shoulder to shoulder, and her arm brushed Lucia's every time she moved it.

"Not big enough," Lucia whispered into her ear for at least the fifth time since they started the game.

Agnete pointed to a large manor in their quarter of the city. "That one?"

Lucia laughed softly into her hair. "Getting warmer," she said. She paused and pointed to an extravagant-looking, multi-story building that Agnete wasn't even sure was a residence. "That one?"

"I don't know... I don't see a little patch for a garden."

"You'd still want a garden?"

"Yes! Of course. I *like* having a garden." She leaned her head on Lucia's shoulder. "...We could move just out of the city," she said. "More space, fewer neighbours... I could have somewhere to plant the clippings from my mother's grave..." she breathed in the scent of Lucia's hair and nuzzled her crown into her neck. "So I could always have a piece of her with me."

"You'd do that?"

"I think so."

Lucia looked at the horizon. "We could build a castle all by ourselves," she said.

"I could grow most of what I need to keep practising witchcraft."

"You could have a *giant* garden. The envy of everyone-" she gasped- "with a *maze*. And rosebushes, as far as the eye can see."

"And a *huge* library."

"Naturally."

"And a whole wing just for guests. Or maybe rescued animals."

Lucia grinned. "Look at you, dreaming so big."

"You're a bad influence on me."

"No, I'm proud of you."

"You would be."

"We could have a ballroom," Lucia continued, "to throw big, extravagant parties. And a conservatory to retreat into when we get tired of hosting said big, extravagant party."

Agnete swallowed. "Or... we could just get a nice home with a fireplace, a little garden, and a cozy nook for a library?"

"It can't be too small," Lucia mused. "I still owe you a child."

"If you wanted... Maybe it could have a couple of extra rooms. For children."

Lucia hummed, the gentle breeze tousling her hair into Agnete's face. She brushed it aside and readjusted herself on Lucia's shoulder. "I think... that *could* be nice," she replied slowly. "You would be the favourite mother, obviously."

"Absolutely not! We'll both be the favourite."

"I don't think you understand how *favourites* work, sweetling."

"You can have two favourites!" she protested. "I'll be the nice one. And you'll be the one that protects them from bullies."

"Ah. The scary one. Of course."

"*And* the one who teaches them how to talk their way into extra food from the stalls on the street. And reads them the best stories at night. And teaches them to dream big and take no disrespect from anyone."

Lucia giggled. "All of that in a little home about-" she pointed to a modest home East of them- "*that* big?"

"Well... *maybe* a little bigger," she relented.

Lucia put her arm around Agnete's back and squeezed her close, planting a deliberate kiss on the top of her head. "I think I could live with that."

-

The hour was late when they started back towards the inn. Steam wafted in filigrees from street vendors' stalls and packs, perpetually dissipating in the lantern light. They wove through the crowds, each waiting for the other to pull them towards their dinner.

Eventually, Agnete guided them towards a vendor selling spiced potatoes and various foods pierced and roasted on long sticks. Agnete approached the vendor and requested her dinner. When she looked back at Lucia, she found her peering into the coinpurse.

"Lucia?"

She raised her head from the pouch at the sound of her name. She looked away. "I'm not actually very hungry," she said, passing a couple of coins to Agnete. "You go on."

She knew that Lucia was lying. She hadn't eaten since her light lunch, well over nine hours ago. Her heart sank as the little metal pieces hit her palm. She only reluctantly gave them to the vendor- they seemed too precious, now.

149

I'll tell her I'm full halfway through, she thought. *Or maybe I'll just tell her that I don't like the potatoes.*

28

Agnete held her shawl folded in her arms- it was kept comfortably warm in the sanitarium. Bart had asked for his daughter, so Lucia had gone to attend to whatever it was that he wanted her attention for. That left Agnete under the loggia, surveying the shrubs planted in clumps in the courtyard.

None of them were therapeutic, as far as she could tell. They were all purely decorative. She couldn't stop herself from souring at what a waste it was. *A garden in the middle of a sick house, and not a single medicinal leaf to be seen. What an unbelievable missed opportunity.*

"Fancy meeting you here."

She turned towards the voice and found Razivia standing behind her. "Good morning," she replied. "How is your husband?"

She affected a shrug of resignation. "As well as can reasonably be expected... How is your father?"

"Oh, no- he isn't my father. He's Lucia's. He's...as well as can be reasonably expected." At least the lies were starting to come more easily. "He took a fall on horseback. He doesn't remember much."

"Of the fall?"

"Of anything."

"Ah... That's a pity." She gave Agnete's arm a gentle squeeze. "That must be a very difficult thing to watch."

She stifled a laugh. "Between you and me," she whispered to the old woman, "He's been much nicer to me since he fell."

Razivia made a high-pitched *tutting* noise. "Is that right?" She chuckled. "I suppose it isn't all bad then, is it?"

"No."

"Well. I'll tell you what." she straightened. "If your old fellow and my old fellow are to be playmates, then we should have tea. There's a lovely little tea house in the South quarter, they know me by name. I regularly meet clients there-"

"That's such a kind invitation," Agnete said, her cheeks flushing. "But... we aren't in a *'teahouse'* position, exactly. In fact, we aren't in much of a position for anything." She overadjusted the shawl in her arms. "We may actually be leaving the city soon... But you're very kind to offer."

Razivia *tsked*. "Well that's rather a pity. It isn't trouble with the law, is it?"

She didn't even lower her voice. "Oh no, it's nothing like that-"

"Just going back home, then?"

"No. Well- not exactly." She hesitated. "When we came here, we only brought so much money. And it... wasn't enough. Not to stay. And we might need to go back, soon. To where we ran from." She didn't mean to say *'ran'*. But it just slipped out.

"Neither of you have found work, then?"

That wasn't a simple matter for either of them. A roof over your head and food on your table cost exponentially more here than it did in the village. As a witch, Agnete would need supplies and time to start practising somewhere new. Lucia, however... Any work she could find in the city wouldn't be nearly enough to support the both of them for any extended time. She would certainly do well working under a Madam, but Agnete knew that Lucia wasn't comfortable with the idea of working in a brothel.

"It's... complicated."

"You could always marry rich."

Agnete chortled. "I supposed that would solve our problems, wouldn't it?"

"That wasn't a joke."

Razivia stared at her impassively. Agnete didn't know how to respond. "...My work makes marriage difficult," she answered limply.

"And your cousin?" When Agnete didn't answer, she said, "I won't pry where I'm not wanted. But she's very beautiful. I'm confident that she could do very well for herself, if she were so inclined. Have her pick of spouses, even. In fact-" she raised her chin- "*If* she likes the idea, then I'll gladly make the arrangements myself. Free of charge." She saw Agnete's confusion. "Friends in high places, hm? I was like you two, once. Us girls have to take care of each other."

"I'm sorry... *'free of charge'*?"

"Oh- my apologies, love. I'm prattling. I probably sound like a snake oil salesman right about now. There's no need for suspicion. *I'm a matchmaker.* The best on this side of the mountains, if I may polish my own brass. If you'd feel better verifying my credentials, I'm happy to offer you some references. I have plenty of happy- *and wealthy-* clients to choose from."

Agnete's throat felt as thought it were starting to close up. Her stomach rippled uncomfortably. "...I would have to ask her," she managed to reply, mouth dry.

"Of course, love. Of course. I'll tell you what-" she reached into a hidden pocket in her skirt and pulled out a small card on heavy paper. Agnete hesitated to take it, fingers hovering around the paper as though it might bite her. "Why don't I host you for tea, myself? I'll give you my address, here. If business comes up in the course of conversation, *lovely*. If not? Then we'll still have a lovely time getting to know one another over sandwiches." She folded Agnete's fingers over the card and smiled. "I'm just an old woman who's grateful for the company."

29

"Razivia invited us over for tea tomorrow."

Lucia perked up. "Did she? That sounds- *wait.*" She turned a sharp eye on Agnete. "Why did you say it like that?"

"Like what?"

"Like there's a catch." Lucia stopped in her tracks, hand still laced with Agnete's and holding her in place. "What aren't you telling me?"

Agnete took a deep breath. "So... just to be clear..."

"Yes."

"This wasn't my own idea. I didn't suggest anything to her. She brought this up entirely on her own-"

"*Agnete.*"

"Well..." she swallowed. "...She's a matchmaker. A very reputable one, to hear her tell it."

Lucia hid her apprehension behind an affected smile. "Don't tell me you're tired of me already, Sweetling."

Agnete pulled Lucia's hand to her lips and kissed her knuckles. "*Never.* But..." She relayed the conversation to Lucia, who listened quietly. "She said that if it doesn't come up, that's fine. She isn't trying to sell you into anything-"

"Perfect. That's that, then."

"...I want you to talk to her about it," Agnete said cautiously. "Just to hear her out."

Lucia opened her mouth and hesitated. When she spoke, it was haltingly. "...Do you not want to be together?" she asked. "Have you changed your mind?"

"No! No, of course I haven't. And I know that this is an unusual thing for me to ask of you... But this could be everything you ever wanted." Catapulting the words into the air didn't soften them as it usually did. This time, it made them feel real. It made them hurt more. "A wealthy, powerful spouse who could give you wealth and power in return, and the opportunities to do anything you want-"

"I want *you*."

"Lucia-" Agnete stepped into her. Her body heat filled the air between them. "*I know you.* You don't have to hide from me. *I love you.* But I know that I'm neither the oldest nor the only dream you have for your life." She saw Lucia's eyes pull focus back into her head, a reflex to avoid meeting Agnete's gaze. Agnete would have been lying if she said that she wasn't pushing in part because she wanted to test her, to see if she would choose Agnete over her ambitions. *But it's not that simple, is it? 'Choosing' one or the other.* Just like it wasn't as simple as denying the woman she loved the chance to have everything she had ever wanted. "I can see you hesitating. And I understand. It's alright. Truly. I can't tell you what your priorities should be. But please... Just hear her out."

If Agnete hadn't have known her as well as she did, she may have missed the hungry glint in Lucia's eyes as she listened to Agnete speak. But she didn't miss it. On the contrary: she had been looking for it. And seeing it made her heart ache.

30

Razivia drew them through the door with all the warmth of an old friend and all the grace of a woman who had spent a lifetime perfecting the art of hosting. Agnete had been anxious since their conversation the previous day. Lucia had been quieter than usual since Agnete implored her to come, which only made her more anxious.

Razivia took them past an immaculately decorated receiving room on the first floor and up a staircase, into a personal sitting room. She hadn't lied about the flowers- there were bouquets of every colour everywhere, two or three full vases per room. Their colours were only made brighter by the cascading greenery thriving in every other corner. The bouquets perfumed each room, sensory attestations of Razivia's skill. They fit seamlessly into the pretty, feminine home.

Agnete had often thought of "luxurious" and "comfortable" as being mutually exclusive. In Razivia's home, she found herself pleasantly surprised.

She poured tea for the two of them from a finely-painted service. She had cream and sugar placed within easy reach on the table. Agnete was the only one who used them. Small sandwiches and quickbreads lay overlapping one another on a tiered tray, along with confections so charming that they triggered something unexpectedly competitive in Agnete.

Razivia said something akin to smalltalk- Agnete hadn't caught it. She was too distracted theorizing how she might be able to replicate the delicate piping on a small fruit-filled cake. Her study was promptly halted by Lucia's direct reply.

"Agnete tells me you're a matchmaker. I'm to understand that you've made us a rather generous offer."

Agnete felt her teeth clench. Lucia had been irritable since they woke up this morning.

Razivia just tittered in response.

"Am I mistaken?" Lucia asked.

"No, love. You just reminded me of myself, just now. When I was still a pretty young thing. Down to the meat of it, I see. You're not mistaken. Your cousin mentioned that you were experiencing some financial difficulties at the moment. I offered my services, free of charge, should you wish to take advantage of them."

"Why me?"

Razivia tilted her head. "Come now, dear. You're a perceptive young woman. You know what you look like."

"Hoping to sell me off to the highest bidder, then?"

"Absolutely not. I'm a matchmaker. Not a slave trader." She reached out and leisurely put a sandwich on her saucer. "Every potential partner I suggest is run by both clients. Under normal circumstances, all of my clients have to pay a fee, which may or may not increase based on a variety of factors. Rarely, however, I'll waive the fee if I feel that someone will do especially well- and if they aren't able to pay, otherwise. There's no need to be proud, dear," she added when she saw Lucia's face. "Life doesn't always deal us a fair hand. And I count myself fortunate to be able to do something I love. If I have the chance to change someone's life for the better, and share my good fortune with others, I rather like to think that I take it." She took a sip of her tea. "Where was I...?"

"Every partner is run by both clients," Lucia answered, more than a little begrudgingly.

"Ah, yes. Thank you. In this particular situation, I would permit you first pick of my suggestions. Should both parties show interest in meeting, I would make the arrangements at a public, neutral location. Unless privacy is requested. In which case, the meeting would happen downstairs in the receiving room, under my discreet supervision. If either party changes their mind at any time, then the match is discarded."

"And how many clients of yours are difficult to match?"

Their host raised a cool eyebrow at Lucia. "I'm not afraid of a challenge, if that's your intended meaning."

"Even if they're only marrying for money or power?"

"Why do you think half of my clients come to me?"

Lucia leaned back in her seat. "It seems rather cruel," she replied icily, "when the other half of your clients are looking for love."

Agnete pressed her knees together. *What are you doing?"* she hissed under her breath. *You're the pot calling the kettle black.*

"Believe you me," Razivia said, unwavering. "I make certain that *everyone's* goals and motivations are abundantly clear to one another from the start. And I'm not too humble to say that, between those seeking security and those seeking love, I've been known to kill two birds with one stone."

"And if I had very high standards? Very specific things I was looking for?"

"You wouldn't be the first, nor the last. And looking like you do, I would suppose that you could afford to have high standards."

"And if I have been married previously?"

"That is more common than you'd think."

"And if I didn't come from a wealthy or respectable family?"

"That won't prevent you from marrying into one."

"If I didn't want to spend a lot of time with my spouse?"

"I have clients whose profession requires them to spend much of their time travelling. Many of them just wish for companionship during the uncommon time that they're home."

"If I wanted the freedom to pursue my own education, or my own profession?"

"That's precisely why many seek to marry into wealth."

"If I had family who needed to live with me?" Agnete tore tiny, agitated pieces off of her slice of quickbread. She knew what was happening. Lucia was challenging her, desperately looking for a good reason to say no. The back of her neck started to feel hot.

"Then I suppose you'll want a spouse with a larger home."

"If I'm insufferably cold and don't want to give or receive physical affection?"

"I have clients who only want someone to talk to. There are many different ways to show affection."

"And If I'm a proper battleaxe who likes to treat her spouse harshly?"

A small smile pulled at the corner of Razivia's lips. "I suspect you'll be surprised to find that there are those who find that trait-" she cleared her throat- *"rather desirable."* She took a modest bite out of her sandwich, waiting until she had finished chewing to speak. "You don't manage to achieve what I have without being able to read people, love. If this isn't something you want, then I'll not try to push you. But if it is, then rest assured, I'm not intimidated by whatever challenges your situation may present. If you have nowhere else to go, then you'd be welcome to stay with me until we find a suitable partner.

That goes for both of you, of course," she added, looking to Agnete. "These walls feel terribly empty without my husband to fill them. I'd certainly be glad of the company." She placed her tea and saucer on the table before her and folder her hands in her lap. "If you'd accept my help, I'm certain that I could find someone you would be *very* happy with."

31

Agnete lay on her side, staring at the wall in the dark. She didn't know how long she had been lying there, unable to sleep.

It wasn't fair.

She didn't care if it was a childish thing to think. She didn't care if it was petulant of her.

It wasn't fair.

She'd heard other people talk about heartbreak. Back when the village's problems still left them desperate enough to seek her out. People would come to her and ask for help: to stop the crying, to dull the ache, to make the empty feeling go away so they could feel something, *anything* again. When they spoke of heartbreak, it sounded like a vicious, violent beast. Like something that hid in the trees, lying in wait. Like something that shot out at you all of a sudden, started tearing into you, and didn't stop. But all of Agnete's heartbreaks had been slow. Her heartbreak wasn't a violent beast. Her heartbreak took its time. Her heartbreak let her see it coming, then wrapped itself around her legs before it started savouring her.

She heard Lucia sigh next to her and felt her weight shift on the mattress. She turned over to face her.

"Hi."

"Hi," she whispered back. Her hand found Lucia's. "I can't sleep."

"Neither can I."

Agnete rolled over and lit the candle on their nightstand. She got up and opened the window, letting cool air into the little room. It was quiet outside. Nearly all of the stalls were closed now, the vendors gone home to their own beds for the night. The scarce smattering of lanterns gave more space for the stars to dangle over the city. She descended to her knees and knelt, leaning on the edge of the bed across from Lucia. The question she knew she had to ask stuck in her throat, refusing to budge in the heavy silence. Lucia hugged her pillow as she regarded her, almost childlike.

Agnete counted down the seconds from five- then ten- until she could force the question from her throat.

"Is the meeting with Razivia keeping you awake?" Lucia's eyes unfocused again. *Hiding.* She didn't answer. "It's alright if it is. I understand."

"Why did you make me go?" she demanded softly. "Why did you make me talk to her?"

"Would you rather I hid it from you?"

"*Maybe.*"

"Even if it meant going back to the village? Back to the suspicion and gossip? With no money, no husband, and a witch who so obviously and helplessly adores you?"

Again, she made no answer.

Agnete reached out and took her forearm, tracing her fingers down her skin until they reached her hand. "I know you can't go back," she said, looking into her palm. "*I know.* And I'd never ask it of you. Not even to keep you with me." She raised her head. "This is everything you've ever wanted."

Lucia's eyes began to glisten. "Everything except you."

Agnete exhaled- her breath quivered as it left her lungs. She slowly shook her head. "You're not going back."

"Neither should you!" Lucia threw the pillow back onto the bed and shimmied closer to Agnete. "We could get a little home together. *Here.* They don't deserve you. I know- *they 'need' you.* But what if they don't?" Her eyes drilled into Agnete's. "No one has been to see you for *ages.* Not a *single person.* Being needed by someone means *nothing* if they aren't willing to call on you."

"You're right," she admitted. "It does."

"Besides- we've both been gone for so long that they may have just assumed we've run away."

"You're right. They may have."

"We can make a trip back whenever you want. You can get the clippings from your mother's grave- you could take anything you wanted. We can make an entire *garden* for her! An entire *shrine!* Anything you want!"

"I could."

"Then why couldn't you stay? Everything we imagined- I know it was just a game, a nighttime daydream to entertain ourselves with- but we can have it! *All of it!* We are so close-"

"And your spouse?"

Lucia faltered. She swallowed. "I was married when we met," she said, resolute. "We grew close, spent time together, in spite of that. We can do it again."

"...In secret."

"Well- maybe not *as* secret as before. The city is so much bigger, it would be easier here-"

"But still in secret," Agnete repeated softly. Lucia's wordless stuttering was all the confirmation she needed. "Then we're right back to where we started."

"But we'll be together. I can marry someone wealthy, who travels for work or isn't around often, and we can have a *life* here!"

Agnete took in her pleading on Lucia's face, her features illuminated in the trembling glow of the candlelight. She wanted to remember her like this, agonizing as it was. She wanted to remember how the light kissed her skin and danced over her hair. She wanted to remember the exact shades it brought out in the crystal shards of her eyes. She wanted to remember what she smelled like behind the melting wax and the threat of early morning frost on the wind.

Fighting the tears as well as she could, she squeezed Lucia's hand between her own. "I love you," she told her. "...But I can't be your secret."

There it was: the one point that couldn't be argued, denied, or persuaded away.

She watched as Lucia's chest started to rise and fall in unsteady waves. The tears fell in rivulets down her cheeks. "But- *you can't-*" she objected. "I still owe you a child-"

"No. No, you don't. I release you. You owe me *nothing.*"

"I don't accept that!"

"It's done. *I release you.* It's done."

"NO."

"We both know," Agnete cooed, stroking Lucia's face with her thumb. *"We both know." We know that sometimes, love just isn't enough.* "I won't be the reason you never get the life you've always wanted."

Lucia weakened. Her voice diminished into something small. *"...But I love you."*

"I love you, too." *That's why I can't hold you back.* Agnete pulled her hand from Lucia's head and held it in front of her chest, little finger extended. "I'll see you under the honeysuckle?"

Lucia's choke rolled into a sob. She grasped Agnete's hand and held it to her forehead, weeping.

32

Agnete made the long journey back to the village alone. She left Lucia in the city with Razivia. She didn't have many belongings to move into the matchmaker's home. Part of her was scared to return to the village... But Lucia and Bart were the only people who had even neared her cottage for ages. She wondered if anyone else had even realized that she was gone.

At Lucia's behest, she took what was left in the coinpurse with her. It was just enough to buy her a couple of hens, a pair of milking goats, and a modest supply of grain in a small town on the way back. It cost less the farther she got from the city. It meant a slower trip back, but she didn't want to risk trying to acquire livestock in the village.

Her home was just as she left it. The barn still had a supply of straw and a half-made pallet bed. There was still a large pile of wood in the woodshed to keep her hearth lit. Herbs she left hung from beams were still tied and strung upside-down, dry and only a faintly fragrant. A book that Lucia had forgotten lay alone by the bed, a leaf jokingly pressed between the pages as a bookmark. Her cups were lined up in their place on the shelf, next to the teapot. One of them was permanently wrapped in a knitted sleeve.

In the days that followed, Agnete prepared herself for confrontation. She didn't know if anyone had realized that she had returned- she hadn't ventured into the village proper. It was hard for her to care if they knew or not. But she did what she could to ready herself: either for a handful of *concerned citizens* to darken her doorstep, or for an angry mob to collect her and demand she answer for Bart and Lucia's disappearance.

No one came.

The days bled into one another as Winter arrived, freezing the ground and sheathing the trees in frost. The days grew darker and colder. The crisp crunch of the leaves coating the forest floor surrendered to the softer, more muffled crunch of snow. Needle-like trees stood skeletal against a sky that looked more and more like the ground flipped upside-down.

Agnete was content to remain in her cottage, letting the village believe that she was long gone. The solitude meant living on porridge, bread, Winter forage, preserves, and whatever eggs and milk she could gather from her newest charges. The animals helped her feel less alone. She would bring them into the cottage sometimes, to give them a little extra warmth and herself a little extra company. It still felt as though no amount of wood in the hearth could banish the chill within or without.

Time slogged on. And still no one came.

-

Agnete debated whether or not to put on her shawl when she finally heard a knock at her door. She was half-expecting to find pitchforks on the other side.

She tepidly pulled it over her shoulders. *Let them be reminded of who cared for them and their families before they drag me away.*

A second knock sounded at the door as she made her way over without the faintest suggestion of speed in her steps.

When she opened it, she remarked with disinterest that there was only one person waiting for her.

"Crona," Friderik muttered, eyes cast downward, "I humbly beg aid of your wisdom."

Agnete stood there, indifferently staring at him.

She felt angry. But not like she had been, before. She didn't feel the slow boil that threatened to erupt from her chest. She couldn't. Part of her felt too sad that even if she did feel that angry- like she might lose herself- that Lucia wasn't there to pull her back.

Maybe that's the secret to not losing control, she thought. *To always be a little too sad to.* Sadness dampened the anger. It slowly suffocated it.

He waited for her to say something or invite him inside. She looked him over- she didn't immediately see anything out of place. *Maybe he just wants a charm or a small spell.* She passively scanned his stance, his hands, his skin... *If he's injured, it must be under his clothes. If he's sick, it must be a malady that can't be seen right away. Or at all.*

"I humbly beg aid of your wisdom," he repeated with greater urgency.

She took a deep, thoughtful breath.

It could be deadly serious. Or it could be nothing.

She would never know until she invited him inside.

She looked him over one last time. She found him looking her in the eye, imploring, perhaps for the very first time.

She met his gaze with her own.

"No."

She stepped back and shut the door in his face.

33

Agnete wandered between the trees, plucking Winter berries from intermittent bushes and putting them in her skirt. She had misplaced her basket, and was left to amble through the woods with her skirt gathered bowl-like in her hand. She took only a little more than she needed- enough to make an extra jar of jam or syrup, but still leave plenty for the birds and squirrels. She gave no thought to the tracks she left in the snow. She didn't need to.

The woods were quiet in the Winter... she had always liked that. It felt peaceful to her. It almost turned the longing of loneliness into something comforting, rather than something to be endured. The snowflakes fell gently from the sky, drifting through the trees, landing in her hair and eyelashes. They floated onto the pile of red berries in her skirt, disintegrating one by one against their smooth flesh.

She made her way back to the cottage with her haul, feet trudging through the thick blanket of snow. As she made her way into the clearing, her legs slowed to a halt.

Lucia stood a distance from the house, on the opposite side of where the vegetable garden would have been.

Agnete blinked. She decided that she didn't really mind, if this was just her mind playing tricks on her. *Solitude is a fickle thing. I don't think I'd be disturbed now, to know that I was conjuring my own companionship.* She cautiously approached her.

She stopped in front of her. Lucia's breath steamed in the air. Her hair was adorned with the same snowflakes as Agnete's. There was a bloom to her cheeks, bright against the monochrome cold.

She was real.

"Hi," Lucia said,

Agnete plunged her hand into her skirt and started hurling handfuls of berries at Lucia.

Lucia's hands flew up as she stumbled backwards in an attempt to defend herself against the attack.

"What are you doing?!" Agnete demanded, shouting over the rock in her throat. *"Why aren't you in the city?!"*

"I brought some things-" Lucia gestured behind her as Agnete ran out of berries to throw. Agnete peered behind her- she hadn't noticed the small cart and the horse. A cover protected several large sacks and a pile of plush-looking textiles from the snow. "It's food, mostly... some blankets... A few books..." She eyed Agnete nervously. "I hope you have room for the horse in the barn..."

Agnete started to catch her breath. "Why are you here?"

Lucia started fiddling with her gloves. "...I tried. I really did. I even wanted it... rather, I *tried* to want it. But Razivia kept finding suitors for me, and I kept meeting them... And she's just as good as she claims. If I had met her before I knew you..."

Agnete drank her in: the fine clothes, the expensive-looking furs, the healthy glow to her skin. This was not the look of a poor woman. "...Are you married, then?" she asked. "Or about to be?" *Or with child already, come to insist on honouring the exchange I released you from?*

Lucia hesitated. For the moment before she spoke, Agnete's stomach dropped into her feet. "...There were a couple of *almosts*," she replied slowly. "People I could have pictured myself content with. You'd be surprised, how many gifts you receive when a person of means- *real* means, not like Bart- is hoping to secure your hand in marriage." She smoothed over her clothes. "It's rather like a business arrangement."

"I didn't think that would bother you."

"It didn't. Not really. But the more I pictured a future with these people, the more my mind kept coming back to that day we bought out half of the shopkeeps in the village-" she betrayed herself with an uncertain giggle- "When you asked me what my perfect future looked like. If everything went exactly how I wanted it to.

"...I was closer to what I thought I wanted than I'd ever been. My entire life, I've been dreaming of wealth and power and freedom... and it was so close that I could reach out and touch it. I could *taste* it. But it just felt like... *ash* in my mouth. Because what then? I-I get everything I want, and... to what end? I *almost* had it. And I didn't feel any happier." Her voice began to waver. "I still felt that *empty, gaping hole* in my chest. The same one that's *always* been there. And I thought of Bart and how he spent his entire life chasing happiness, and Agnete, I have *never* been satisfied. *Never in my life,* and you- you made me feel like that gaping hole inside me wasn't so big-"

Agnete closed the distance between them and wrapped Lucia in her arms.

"The one thing I knew about myself," she continued into Agnete's shoulder, "without a second thought, was that I was a woman who knew *exactly* what she wanted out of life. But... I don't think I know what I want out of life, anymore," she sobbed.

Agnete held her tighter. "It's alright. We can figure it out together. We have all the time in the world."

"I feel like I don't know who I am, anymore."

"You're my fox."

Lucia made a whimpering sound against her. "I don't know what to do," she whispered.

"Here's what we're going to do." Agnete nuzzled her head against her and pulled away, just enough to see her face. "We're going to get this beautiful horse into the barn and introduce them to their new friends. We're going to pick up these berries and bring everything on that cart into the house and out of the snow. I'm going to make you a pot of your favourite tea and wrap you in every last blanket I own. I'm going to bake you a fresh batch of those nut cookies you loved. I'm going to warm a cup of milk for you. I'm going to hold you for as long as you need me to, and then a little bit longer. I'm going to boil you a hot bath and brush your hair. I'm going to read you any book you want when you're ready to fall asleep. And in the morning, I'm going to make you cinnamon rolls for breakfast." She took Lucia's head in her hands. "We're going to spend the Winter here, together. And then we're going to decide where we want to go when the sun returns."

Lucia looked at her, red-eyed and defenceless. She pulled Agnete in and kissed her, melting into her as though she had finally come home.

When she pulled away, Agnete brushed a lock of Lucia's hair back behind her ear and smiled. "People like you need people like me to protect them."

Acknowledgements

Planner that I am, I've made a mental list of everyone I wanted to thank on this page. But now that I sit here, days away from publication, I find myself unsure of how to start.

I want to thank my beta readers, as they would like to be named: *Milu M.*, *Evening Starlight*, *Furiosa Le Fay*, and *Her Ladyship*. Every piece of feedback you have given me has helped me see this book from a new perspective and craft it into a better story. For your honesty, your time, and your enthusiasm: Thank you.

I want to thank my cover photographer, Galina Afanaseva, for the unequivocally stunning cover photo. Working with you was an absolute pleasure- thank you for taking my vague idea and turning it into something beautiful.

I want to thank Isabel O. for all of her help with cover design and arrangement. Your eye is far more keen than mine- I am so grateful for your readiness to lend it.

I want to express a very sincere and nonspecific thanks to every single person who, at any point, has expressed interest or given me encouragement about my writing. It's the cumulative effect of all of these small sentiments that helped push me here.

Finally, I want to thank *you.*
Yes, *you.*
Whether you purchased this book at full price and devoured it from cover to cover, or whether you simply stumbled upon it in a dilapidated cardboard box marked *"FREE"* and figured, "What the hell? May as well."
Don't misunderstand me: I wrote this for myself.

But I refined it, polished it, and made every effort to make it beautiful for *you*.

I hope it stays with you for the rest of your life.

(Even if you hated it.)

(Perhaps especially *if you hated it.)*

Syren Nightshade *(she/her)* is a Canadian writer, dancer, singer, actress, and performing artist. She has an affinity for Gothic fiction, and frequently explores themes of feminine rage, longing, & duality in the pages of her work.

Meet Me Under the Honeysuckle has been her first experimental foray into self-publishing.